THE CASE OF THE HEADLESS BILLIONAIRE

A totally gripping, breathlessly twisty crime mystery

MICHAEL LEESE

Detectives Roper and Hooley Mysteries Book 1

Originally published as
Going Underground

Revised edition 2021
Joffe Books, London
www.joffebooks.com

First published by in Great Britain in 2017
as *Going Underground*

Cover art by Nick Castle

ISBN: 978-1-78931-926-2

PROLOGUE

Six weeks earlier

David Evans looked at the familiar face of his personal assistant, Sylvia Gale. It was the weekend, but he wasn't surprised she had come to work. He returned her smile, thinking again how lucky he was to have her.

"Sorry to interrupt you, Mr Evans," she said. He would always be Mr Evans, despite his gentle efforts to get her to call him David over the twenty-five years or so they had been together. He was a successful solicitor who had done well from the property boom, but he was sure that if she ever left, then part of his business would depart with her.

He glanced down at his tie. He always wore a shirt and tie, even at the weekend. His wife teased him for being stuffy, but she liked the way it demonstrated a commitment to doing things in the traditional way. Today she had picked out a light-blue shirt with a blue-striped tie. She thought the combination suited his ruddy complexion, pale-blue eyes and grey hair. The sound of Sylvia's voice brought him back to the present, and Evans realised he had allowed his mind to wander, leaving his PA waiting for a reply.

"I said, would you like a cup of tea?" she repeated, not appearing to be irritated. She knew he was possessed of an imagination that snatched him away from the real world. Like her boss, Sylvia always made an effort to dress appropriately, as she liked to think of it. Today she was wearing her standard office outfit of a black skirt, loose-fitting white blouse, which she used to try and disguise an ample bosom, dark stockings and dark loafers that were solid and comfortable. Balanced on the tip of her nose were her new tortoiseshell glasses, purchased after grudgingly accepting that she could no longer see her computer screen. Evans thought they suited her, but he kept that to himself as he knew she hated them. Her make-up was minimal, and her hair looked as though she had just come from the salon — which she had. She always had her hair done first thing on a Saturday.

Evans ran his hand through his own hair. It was a habit his wife said had got worse since it started falling out. She claimed he was continually checking he still had some. He didn't know about that, but he was happy to admit that he longed for the thick brown mop he had taken for granted in his younger days.

He switched from thoughts of his youth to the needs of today. "Tea would be delightful, but you really don't need to be here, you know. How is your mum, by the way?"

She seemed to shrink into herself for a moment — or was that his imagination? "She's been better the last few days. It seems to go up and down. But she's well enough for me to leave her with one of our neighbours, at least for a couple of hours. It gives me the chance to get out of the house. It can get a bit claustrophobic. Anyway, I can always be back there in ten minutes."

He thought "claustrophobic" might be something of an understatement but knew better than to push the point. "You know best, of course, and I understand the need to take a break from family life."

She left the room, and he returned his attention to his computer. He was spending more time in the office at weekends so he could indulge in his hobby. He caught himself. This was more than just a hobby, it was his passion, and it was increasingly dominating his thoughts. He had always enjoyed his work as a solicitor, and over the years he had steadily built up his suburban practice. But it had all got a little predictable, so this provided the mental challenge he was looking for. At sixty-two, he was already considering retiring, and this new project would more than adequately help him fill the time. He had even started taking on the odd commission and had just completed an especially challenging task that had taken up many of his days off. Today he was reviewing his work. It was easy to make mistakes, but he was a perfectionist.

Ten minutes later, he was deep in his research again, and this time he didn't even look up as he heard his PA backing through his door holding a tray in her hands. His office could have come straight from a museum about 1950s England. Polished brown furniture dominated, and he sat at an elegant high-backed captain's chair, finished with green leather, in front of a large oak desk. On the client's side were two comfortable chairs that were almost old enough to be classified as antiques. The carpet, an ancient Axminster that had probably done thirty years' service, was light brown with thin green thread woven in for contrast. Against one wall was a row of gun-metal-grey cabinets, and on the wall above them was a picture of the queen taken on her silver jubilee. It only lacked a Bakelite radio tuned to the Home Service. Betraying the present day were his flat-screen monitor, printer, shredder and mobile phone — an iPhone, because his children had told him it was the best.

Sylvia turned carefully as she made it through the door then crossed to the desk, where she placed her tray on the dark-green leather surface. She'd done this hundreds, maybe thousands, of times before. The tray held tea made just the way he liked it: loose-leaf English breakfast in a Brown Betty pot that had been carefully warmed before the tea leaves were covered in freshly boiled water and left to brew for four minutes. Gale placed a strainer over the white, bone-china cup, with matching saucer, and poured out his drink; the milk went in afterwards, not before. She leaned across the desk to place the cup within easy reach of his right hand. On other days, there might have been a plate of biscuits, but Evans had promised his wife that he would lose a few pounds.

So far, she had followed the routine exactly. But now she did something different. She lifted a white cloth from the tray to reveal a Smith & Wesson M66 Combat Magnum. It was loaded with .38 Special rounds, rather than the more normal .357 Magnum cartridges. It had been explained to Sylvia that this was probably one of the most straightforward guns to handle. It was said to combine effective stopping power with simplicity of use. The choice of ammo was also supposed to help. Slightly less recoil. Marginal gains. She was told this was the way to go for a first-timer. The one thing they kept repeating was: just one shot, that's all you'll get. Don't expect to get a second. When it came to the real thing, she would start to panic; everyone did. This would throw off her aim, making it unlikely she would hit the target twice. Now she picked up the gun and started to take aim. At that moment, something alerted Evans. Maybe her ragged breathing. He looked up to see his PA standing there with a gun.

Flight, fight or freeze — the primary responses to fear. Evans froze. He was so astounded he didn't take in that she had adopted a textbook shooting position. Knees slightly flexed, one foot placed slightly ahead of the other, taking her weight on the balls of her feet. But there were two things he couldn't miss. The gun was pointing at him, and her finger was starting to exert pressure on the trigger.

1

One month earlier

London traffic could be unbearable, even if you were experiencing it from the luxurious back seat of a Rolls-Royce Phantom. When it was slow-going like this, Sir James Taylor enjoyed a game of his own devising: watching cyclists present the finger as they weaved past. While they couldn't see in through the rear privacy glass, it was a reasonable assumption that a City fat cat might be lurking inside. To win the game, he had to guess how many fingers he would see on any given trip. Get it right, and he would treat himself to a glass of champagne at home. Guess wrong, and he would donate £500 to charity. So far, the champagne remained unopened, and the cost was mounting. He didn't mind. If you could afford a car like this — it was the Mark VIII version and worth north of £400,000 with a few customised finishes — you could afford to pay your debts.

But in the last half an hour, the car had managed to move forward about three feet, and he had already lost. The number of fingers had gone above and beyond his prediction. Not even the soothing tones of Vivaldi floating out of the hand-built stereo system could ease his mounting impatience as he stared at an unchanging view of Fleet Street from the Ludgate Hill end.

"Traffic seems particularly bad tonight, Adam," he said to his driver.

"Yes, sir," he replied, nodding at the satnav screen. "This is telling me there's been a student demonstration in Westminster. They've managed to grid-lock the area, so it's causing problems all over Central London."

Sir James snorted. "What are they moaning about now? Someone asked them to hand in the annual essay?"

The driver's shoulders shook slightly as he suppressed a laugh. He always tried to remain the cool professional when he was working, but Sir James had a wickedly sly sense of humour. He glanced in his rear-view mirror and saw his boss undoing his seatbelt.

"Getting out, sir?"

"Yes. I can't stand any more of this. I need a bit of exercise, so might as well walk home from here. It's a decent trot to Eaton Square and might help me shed a few pounds."

The driver thought that if Sir James lost any more weight, he'd be positively skinny, but kept that idea to himself.

"You might as well call it a day. I won't need you again until tomorrow morning at the usual time."

With that, he opened the door and stepped out onto the pavement. There was a burst of sound from the street — the rumbling of car engines, and pedestrians talking, laughing and cursing at cyclists and vehicles. The noise was accompanied by the thick, hot smell of engine fumes generated by so many idling engines. Then the tumult was shut out as the door closed with an almost imperceptible clunk. From his incredibly comfortable seat behind the wheel, the driver watched his boss walk past the Punch Tavern and then disappear into the crowds near a sign pointing to St Bride's Church. He left it a few minutes to make sure he wasn't going to change his mind and then pulled off his peaked cap. With a bit of luck, someone might even think the car belonged to him. Now all he had to do was work out how he was going to get out of this traffic jam and back to the secure underground car park at Canary Wharf, where his own Nissan Micra was currently occupying a small corner of the Rolls's parking place.

2

Present day

The thick file thumped down on his desk, making Chief Inspector Brian Hooley jump. Once again his boss, Deputy Assistant Commissioner Julie Mayweather, had surprised him.

"As light on your feet as ever, ma'am," he said.

A hint of a smile touched her brown eyes, but her expression was deadpan.

"Sir James Taylor," she said, nodding at the file.

He felt a sudden spike of interest. "The billionaire that's been missing for a week now?"

"Nearly two, actually, and not anymore. He's been found — or some of him has." Responding to her deputy's raised eyebrow, she added, "They found a torso a week back. The head and limbs had been cut off. Made it bloody difficult to ID him, but they managed yesterday. Everything you need to know is in there. Come and see me once you've gone through it."

With that, she turned on her heel and left his office as silently as she had entered, her feet seeming to glide over the carpeting. Hooley closed the document he'd been studying on his computer. Then he started on the material in front of him. He was pleased it was a physical copy, being of an age where paper beat the screen every single time.

An hour later and he had a clear picture in his mind. Based on what he had just read, Sir James was a man who gave capitalism a good name. He'd started out as a trader and then rapidly set up his own hedge fund, making billions for himself and his investors through specialising in what was described as ethical investments. The sort where some attempt was made to share profits around and not deal with despots. Five years ago, his wife had died after a short but brutal battle with breast cancer. He took two months off to mourn her death and then announced he was quitting the financial world. Instead, he was going to use his fortune to help others.

He created a charity in his wife's name, the Miriam Foundation, and set about giving his money away. Since he had so much, it was going to take a long time. Unsurprisingly, breast cancer charities were among the early beneficiaries, but he also donated large sums to children's and fertility causes. He and his wife had never been able to have their own, despite it being their dearest wish. He was exceptionally generous to scientists and doctors involved in new techniques to aid conception. A year ago, his work was rewarded with a knighthood. It was an obvious high point, but Hooley thought it must have also reminded him of how much he missed his wife and how proud she would have been to come to Buckingham Palace to see the queen tap his shoulders with the sword.

Then he had vanished. He was last seen by his driver, who'd picked him up from a board meeting at the foundation's headquarters in Canary Wharf. Those present said he had been in an ebullient mood, identifying some new recipients for donations and paying attention to various reports. The meeting had wrapped up shortly before 5 p.m. Sir James had declined a drink, saying he was heading home and looking forward to eating a shepherd's pie prepared by his housekeeper, by all accounts an excellent cook. She had made it that morning and left it in the fridge for when he got home.

The housekeeper was the first to raise the alarm. The following morning, she arrived for work at 7 a.m. as usual. Checking the fridge, she noted that the food was untouched. She went upstairs and realised he had not used the bed in his suite of rooms on the second floor. She looked outside to see that the driver was already there with the Rolls-Royce. He told her that he had assumed Sir James was inside as he had last seen him being swallowed up by crowds of pedestrians thronging Fleet Street the previous evening. He had taken to walking a lot since his wife died, partly because it kept him fit, but also because it helped fill the time.

For the next few hours, Judith Kelly had waited anxiously for news — Sir James was usually the most predictable of people — then decided to check with the foundation. This sparked off a chain of phone calls, all of which revealed the same thing: no one could get hold of him. Just before 1 p.m. an increasingly anxious PA had called the police. For the first couple of hours it had been treated as a routine missing person's report, but over the next 48 hours, it was rapidly bumped up in importance, eventually landing in the lap of a Superintendent John Williams. Hooley had worked with the man and knew he was a good officer, and so it proved. His team did everything by the book, including an appeal which generated press coverage around the world. It's not every day that a billionaire goes missing.

But as the days went on the mystery deepened. The last person known to have seen him alive was the driver, who found his world turned upside down as police examined every aspect of his life. An equally sharp focus was set on the housekeeper, his PA and the foundation board. This also revealed nothing. It was as though he had disappeared from the face of the earth. Every possibility was considered, and given that he had got out of a car near the River Thames, CCTV footage covering Blackfriars Bridge was checked and re-checked in case he had jumped. The river police were put on high alert, but no body was found.

The only slight oddity which had emerged was that Sir James had created his own DNA profile. It was not something he had ever discussed with colleagues. Still, it was assumed he had done it because he might have been thinking about needing specialised treatment at some stage in the future. Whatever the reason, it was this that eventually led to the identification of his body.

Three weeks into the search, in an apparently unrelated incident, the torso of a man had been found in the cellar of a disused warehouse in East London. By then, Supt. Williams had issued an instruction that any unidentified body should have its DNA taken and the details passed immediately to his squad. In this case, there had been a slight delay because the mortuary where the body ended up was understaffed and over-worked. But yesterday the news had come in that the partial remains were those of the missing billionaire.

As he finished reading, Brian Hooley sighed and sat back in his chair. His eyes felt gritty, and he rubbed at them to try and get some relief. A thirty-year veteran of the Met, he knew when trouble was heading his way. He picked up one of the pictures that were included in the notes. Holding it in his right hand, he was struck that even in a photograph, Sir James radiated a powerful aura. He was clearly a man used to taking centre stage, and he looked the part. His perfectly cut salt-and-pepper hair and silver-rimmed glasses complemented his pink-cheeked complexion. He thought wryly that the suit Sir James was wearing almost certainly cost more than he earned in a month. He carefully replaced the photo in the file and made his way to his boss's office.

3

Hooley was surprised his backside wasn't imprinted on the faux-leather seat of the chair in front of Mayweather's desk. He'd spent enough time sitting there over the years. His boss watched as he settled in and then absent-mindedly took off her reading glasses as she leaned forward. She was wearing her usual outfit of a formal white blouse, a black tie and her light-weight dress uniform.

"What do you think?" she said, placing her small hands on the desk.

He noted she looked fit and focussed, and it reminded him that he'd let things slip a little since his wife had thrown him out. Maybe he should start walking up the stairs again. It was five floors to the incident room near Victoria Station, so that would help. And maybe stick to white wine rather than pints of lager.

He brought himself back to the moment. They'd worked together long enough not to rush each other. Both operated best when they had time to think.

"Between us," he said, shrugging, "I think this may turn out to be a hospital pass. The investigation so far looks first-rate; the chances of us finding something new are pretty slim. I fear we might end up looking like hapless plods." He scratched the tip of his nose before continuing. "As far the public is concerned, the identification of the body is the perfect moment for a new team to take over, review the excellent work already done and make significant progress in resolving what has proved to be a frustrating case."

This time there was more than the hint of a smile in her eyes as she nodded her appreciation of his comments. "I think you should write down that 'perfect moment' stuff and send it to the press people. It might help them spin this into a success story."

Mayweather then steepled her hands under her chin and shook her head slightly. "The trouble is it's our problem now. Once the ID came in about the body, Sir James's friends were able to get to the PM. He called the home secretary to ask what was going on; the home secretary called the commissioner to put the squeeze on, who in turn passed responsibility to his chief of staff. Then I got the call. To be fair to Hugh Robertson, even though he was steaming, he only shouted at me briefly. If I remember correctly the actual phrase used was, 'You're the Special Investigation Unit — so do something special and find out what's happened.'"

Hooley nodded. Despite his earlier comments he accepted the missing billionaire was now his responsibility and was already thinking about what they would need to do. Which probably meant doing everything all over again if he was any judge. At least now they had a body and a location to work with.

"Right. We need to treat this as a new case so we can start re-interviewing everyone, beginning with the chauffeur and housekeeper. Let's see if anything has shaken loose since they were last spoken to." He was gently clicking his fingers as he counted off the tasks. "I think I might go and talk to the guy who found the body again. I'm not saying he did it, but what was he up to in there? That warehouse was, as far as he knew, empty. All he was supposed to do was check the locks, but he said he could smell something and went back.

"William's team says it's a solid old structure and the body was in a deep cellar at the very back. Our man must have an acute sense of smell to have picked something up from outside and through a locked door . . . I wouldn't be at all surprised if he was looking for a little out-of-the-way place to store some items that might have fallen off the back of a lorry.

"The reports say it took twenty minutes before he stopped throwing up enough to complete the 999 call. They've got call records of him trying three times and breaking off to be sick. That'll teach him to go around opening body bags he stumbles over in dark cellars in the East End."

He grinned, feeling pleased with himself. "It's got to be worth putting the squeeze on him to see if anything pops. If we get all that going and put DS Toni Barton on drawing up a detailed case plan, at least we'll be covering all the bases. But my concern is that we'll have slim pickings to choose from."

Mayweather, who had been silent throughout Hooley's speech, put her glasses back on then carefully pushed them down her nose. She had a habit of looking over the top of the frames and making eye contact while she was thinking.

"You're right about that, and in fact, the warehouse is an oddity — the way ownership is hidden behind layers of offshore companies. Maybe it's somebody waiting to cash in on property prices, but I don't like it when things are secret." She paused and gave him another one of her looks. "What's your take on his head and limbs being missing?"

Hooley took a deep breath. It was one of the issues that most troubled him. "It certainly slowed down identification. The initial report says the amputations, for want of a better word, were very clean and precise. I might be persuaded that this indicates a professional killing — planned, rather than a crime of passion or a spur-of-the-moment thing.

"I also wonder if we'll ever find the other bits of the body. One of my mates heard a whisper that some undertakers turn a blind eye to the odd bit of extra baggage in a coffin, especially for cremation. In the world we live in, who knows? It's sort of, 'Here are the remains of Tom, Dick and Harry.'"

Mayweather suppressed a shudder. She wasn't an especially religious woman, but she had long ago learned that respect for the dead was vital. Police officers often deployed black humour to help keep the awful things at bay. Still, in any murder, you were looking at a human being, with all the relationships that entailed.

She looked out through her office door and across to the large incident room, her gaze drawn to the digital wall-clock that showed it was past 7 p.m. They needed to wrap up for the day. They were going to have a lot to do tomorrow.

"Anything else of immediate interest, Brian?"

He took another deep breath.

"I think we should get Roper back in."

Mayweather took her glasses off and held his gaze for several seconds.

"Are you sure? I can still vividly remember what happened last time. That was almost a disaster."

"I know, and I'm not defending him for that. But he's paid the price and learned some very tough lessons. He's never going to be the life and soul of the party, but you just need to give him space. So what that he doesn't get the social niceties? While everyone else is wishing each other 'good morning', he's ploughing through the reports and spotting the hidden clues. Most people understand that about him and make allowances. We can't all be the same. It would be rubbish if we were."

Despite her DI's surprisingly heartfelt defence of Roper, Mayweather still looked doubtful.

Before she could say anymore, he jumped in. "You don't need to decide tonight. Let's talk again tomorrow once things are underway. Maybe I can go and see how he is. If I have any doubts, I'll tell you straight away."

He looked away for a moment, and she wondered if he was apprehensive. Was he more concerned about bringing Roper back than he was letting on? She knew that he felt a sense of unfinished business there and hoped that wasn't his main motivation.

Hooley made his way out, turning in the doorway for a final plea. "We really need his help."

4

"How can you tell what someone's thinking?" Jonathan Roper was wearing his trademark outfit of black suit, white shirt and black tie. His curly, black hair was as unruly as ever, as though he had just walked through a wind tunnel, even though there was no breeze at all. He had large brown eyes that could shine with energy and a pale complexion.

The DCI smiled. Typical opening from Roper, no time wasted on saying hello.

"Lovely to see you again, Jonathan. I must say you're looking well."

Roper thought for a moment. "Sorry," his gaze drifted down to his super-shiny black shoes. "I'm trying to remember all that stuff. It's been 92 days since we last met in person. I'm feeling well, although you seem to have put on a bit of weight."

This statement was accompanied by him staring at Hooley's stomach, which the DCI had to admit had expanded. He waited until Roper was looking up again.

"Can you tell what I'm thinking now?" he asked with narrowed eyes.

Roper was oblivious. "Of course not," he said with a shake of his head. "That's why I was asking you just now if you could tell me how to do it."

Hooley sighed and told himself to get on with it. "You can never know what people are really thinking. But there are clues. For example, if you tell someone they look fat and then stare at their stomach, you may notice they get cross."

Roper looked perplexed. "But if I started piling on the pounds, I would want to know straight away, and then I could do something about it. When I saw how fat you were looking, I had to say something."

Hooley just stopped himself from giving him a death-stare. Trying to explain human emotions to Roper was a complex exercise.

They were standing outside the building on the South Bank of the River Thames, where Roper lived in a three-bed-roomed penthouse with wonderful views. Tower Bridge was to the left and the financial district of Canary Wharf over to the right. The area looked spectacular at night with all the buildings' lights. Now it was just after 6 p.m., and crowds of home-going commuters were dodging around them. Mostly pedestrians, but also a good sprinkling of runners and the odd cyclist using the pavement as a bypass.

Hooley had called earlier that day to fix the meeting after Mayweather, a little reluctantly, had agreed that he should see Roper. Ignoring the predictable lack of social skills, first impressions were positive. He looked well and had replaced the weight that had dropped alarmingly before the incident took place. For a man once described as having the physique of a pipe cleaner, that was a good thing. But it was the bigger picture that was reassuring. Today he was calm and engaged. He knew that Roper had been working with a support group for autistic people, which seemed to be helping him relax.

"Come on, let's get inside, and you can tell me what you've been up to for the last 92 *days*," he said, thinking only someone like Roper would know exactly how many days it was.

They stepped out of the lift and Roper bounded ahead. Stopping at his door, he turned with an expectant expression. Hooley realised there had to be something new, and it took him a moment before he spotted it.

"Iris recognition system. I'm seriously impressed. Are you storing gold bars in there?"

Roper was already bending slightly to line his eye up with the lens. There was a bit of flashing light and then a click. He pushed the door open and walked inside. Hooley grinned to himself, in the same circumstances, many people would have mimed a flourish to encourage their guests inside. Not Roper. See open door, walk through open door.

"Never have to worry about losing my keys or forgetting to take them with me." Roper was obviously delighted with his new toy. The older man decided that whatever the cost it was a good investment. He'd lost track of the times Roper had needed to call in a locksmith to get into his own flat. Leaving a spare key under the mat wasn't really an option around here unless you wanted all and sundry popping in. He thought it was one of life's mysteries: how could a man who seemed so organised manage to consistently lose things?

Roper headed straight for the fridge and pulled out a bottle of Hooley's favourite lager, plus a bottle of white wine. "I went shopping as soon as you rang, so which one of these would you like?"

The DCI noted the beguiling frosting effect on the beer, thought about the wine, dismissed the idea of a coffee then took in the warm sunshine bathing the balcony and looked at the beer again. He bowed to the inevitable, lightly dismissing his weakness as appropriate behaviour in the circumstances. It would have been rude not to accept a beer after Roper had gone to the effort of buying it. The DCI poured his drink into a glass, then held it up to the light to appreciate the colour. Only then did he take a sip.

"You not having one?"

"I might do later, but I thought that I could read your mind just now. I knew you were going to go for the beer." He pulled a face that showed his frustration. "I can do things like that with you but not with other people."

"Well, you do know me very well, and I take it the look on my face, and the way I stared at the bottle, gave me away."

Hooley took another long swig of his beer as they moved outside. He leaned on the balcony railing and watched a large commuter boat swish past heading downriver towards Greenwich. Inside he'd kept the conversation light, but now he wanted to probe a little deeper.

"So, why has guessing what people are thinking moved top of your agenda?"

"Because the counsellor told me I needed to work on body language and being empathetic, which means I have to try and put myself in the other person's position."

The DCI allowed himself to think about that. After things went tits up last time, the HR people at Scotland Yard had insisted that if Roper was going to work for them again, he needed to take some courses and undergo counselling. Hooley had argued this was unnecessary. Most people accepted Roper as he was, a hard-working colleague who got things done. Only a small minority found his little "quirks" a barrier.

"I'm not sure that's the best advice for you. I really don't think empathy is your thing. I don't mean that in a bad way, you do try to get on with people, but for you, it's a bit different. Or at least that's what I think.

"I know plenty of decent coppers who have the empathy of a house brick, and no one's telling them to go around reading peoples' minds, so I don't see why you should have to. And anyway, if I could read minds, there'd be no more crime."

He'd always had a soft spot for the enigmatic Roper, and a bond of mutual trust had grown between them. To be honest, he'd missed the younger man's idiosyncratic approach following his suspension.

"Have you done all the courses they asked you to do?"

A quick nod of the head. "I finished those a month ago, and the counsellor says he's taken things as far as he can. He said I should only see him again if I really need him. He said that several times."

Now Hooley was grinning. He could imagine the counsellor was hoping he'd seen the back of his new client, especially if each session turned into a brain-stretching discussion about empathy and how it worked.

"For what it's worth, I never thought you needed any of that. You know my view: you need to be patient with people when they can't keep up. Try saying hello when you answer the phone, remember to say please and thank you when people do things for you and try to notice when people are talking to you or asking questions."

They were both silent as they watched all the activity on the river, then Hooley turned to Roper. "Two more questions then I'm done. First question, what are you going to do if you get carried away again?"

"Talk to you first, before I do anything."

Hooley extended his hand.

"Excellent. When do you want to come back to work?"

There was a pause. "Was that the second question?"

"It was."

"Then I'd like to start straight away."

5

"So, you're convinced." Mayweather tapped one of the files in front of her with a perfectly manicured but unvarnished index finger. "I see he got top marks in the courses we sent him on. I suppose that's a good thing."

Hooley looked sceptical. "I think they were a waste of time, a bureaucratic box-ticking exercise." Realising she was about to interject, he pressed on. "What impressed me is that he really has learned his lesson. He knows he screwed up, and I believe him when he says it won't happen again. Once he gets the point, he doesn't need telling twice, which is a lot more than you can say about most people."

He'd been watching Mayweather while he was talking. Long experience told him she was not yet convinced.

"I still get flashbacks of when he tried to perform a citizen's arrest on that gang leader. He was just lucky we had one of our more sensible people on the observation team and he was able to stop him."

Hooley held his hands up. "I made mistakes in the run-up to the incident. I should have realised that the hours he was putting in were warping his judgement. I found out later that he was regularly going without sleep."

"I don't think you should take the blame, Brian."

"I'm big enough and ugly enough," he smiled. "The point is, I think we've all learned lessons. I need to make sure I keep more of an eye on him. My new office is big enough for another desk. He can work alongside me, which means he can talk to me as and when he comes up with an idea. Which he will do."

Mayweather raised her eyebrows at that last comment. "Just be careful he doesn't drive you mad with his enthusiasm. Get him to come and see me before he starts."

As Hooley made his way out of her office, she called out, "You know the rest of the team started calling him Clouseau?"

He smiled. It could have been worse.

Sitting back at his own desk, he admitted to himself that he was taking a gamble, but he felt the odds were in his favour. The man was the most extraordinary investigator he had ever worked with. Every instinct was telling him that Roper's skills were going to be needed on this case.

He considered the practical problems. The biggest concern was the moment Roper came back to the incident room. He needed his own space, and giving him a desk in Hooley's own office took that pressure away. Maybe he was more like Roper than he realised. He shrugged. He certainly shared the younger man's single-minded approach to catching criminals. As he'd said to Mayweather, he was too long in the tooth to worry about such things. He leaned forward and gently rubbed his temples. Why did life have to be so complicated? Then he grinned. The answer was obvious. Life would be bloody boring if it always made sense.

* * *

Roper sat quietly in front of Julie Mayweather. She had planned to play the video recording of the moment he'd lost the plot, but he was looking so enthusiastic she didn't have the heart to do it.

The footage had been taken by the surveillance team watching a house owned by a man Roper had identified as the leader of a paedophile gang. Thanks to Roper's efforts they had established he was the spider sitting at the centre of a web of crime.

When police had officially arrested the man, they found tens of thousands of images and a mountain of evidence proving he was behind the rape and murder of dozens of children. Closing the case had proved one of the biggest successes for the Special Investigation Unit, but it had nearly turned into an utter fiasco.

Brian Hooley had told her that Roper had put weight back on, but she thought he would always be skinny. He looked as though he needed a good meal, but in fact, he ate an astonishing amount of all types of food and never gained an ounce. He said it was because he had excellent metabolism. Mayweather thought it owed a great deal to the nervous energy he expended.

But looking at him now, she agreed with her deputy that, all things considered, he was in much better shape than a short while ago.

She cleared her throat. "I asked you to see me today because I need to formally welcome you back, and there are a couple of things I need to say before I can do that."

Roper was nodding so eagerly she almost laughed.

"The most important is: you do realise that you can't go around arresting people? You're an investigator — a very good one, and that's why you're attached to my team — but you are not a policeman."

The nodding was now very vigorous.

She thought of the things she could say, how the Crown prosecutors had said that he had nearly wrecked a multi-million-pound investigation. She sighed.

"Go on, get out of here and go and bother the chief inspector." She held up her right index finger as he stood, wanting to add one more thing. "It's good to have you back. We've missed that amazing brain of yours."

6

"You impressed the boss, then?" Hooley was sitting behind his desk. Roper was studying him closely, clearly hoping to read something into the DCI's expression. Hooley decided to help him, and pointed in the direction of his own chin. "This is the look of someone who is both pleased and relieved. I was pretty hopeful she'd have you back, but you can never be sure." He paused for a moment. "I thought we'd agreed that trying to work out what people are thinking is a waste of time."

Roper looked bashful. It was ironic that someone who struggled to work out body language was himself an open book.

"Sorry. I am trying to stop, but I think a part of me keeps hoping that if I try hard enough, I'll be able to do what other people do."

Hooley could think of no answer to that, so he quickly steered the conversation onto work. He pointed at the newly installed desk.

"That's you," said the DCI with a nod. "The tech team says you're still on the system, so you can log on straight away. Once you've had a bit of time to read in, we can talk."

Sitting down, Roper cast a quick glance around the room. It was just the way he liked things: clean and tidy with minimal clutter, nothing that would distract him from his job. He and Hooley were alike in that way. The DCI was not a sentimental man and had no pictures of his family on display, keeping them in a drawer instead. But he did have one of his dog — a large, overweight black Labrador. The dog was apparently smiling at the camera, his large pink tongue flopping out of the side of his mouth.

Roper spent the rest of the morning reading and memorising the police reports and then trawled the internet as he built an ever-expanding profile of Sir James and his charity work. Over the next few days, he would build in more detail and lengthen the timeline, but for now, he was focussing on the last couple of years. Around lunchtime, his thoughts were interrupted by Hooley's voice.

"Do you fancy going to get coffee and a couple of sandwiches for us? I'll have an Americano with milk and whatever you think looks best to eat," he said, brandishing a £20 note at Roper. "My treat to welcome you back, so get whatever you want, and then after we've eaten, let's have a quick review."

Fifteen minutes later Roper was back with the drinks, a smoked salmon on brown for Hooley, and two chicken and avocado sandwiches for himself. Despite having double the amount of food, he still finished eating first.

Finally, the DCI wiped his hands on the paper napkin.

"Good choice that, Jonathan. They do make a delicious smoked salmon."

Roper smiled, Brian Hooley always said the same thing after eating that sandwich.

"Right," said the DCI, "you go first."

Roper took a quick breath and then launched into his assessment.

"I agree with what you told me yesterday. There's no obvious reason why anyone would want to kill him. There's no suggestion of anything controversial happening in his business affairs or any hint of a dispute. In fact, he hasn't been involved in any business deals for quite some time. His entire focus has been on his charitable foundation."

He got to his feet, and began to pace up and down in front of Hooley. Although the DCI wasn't fazed by his habit of walking around while talking, he was aware that a few members of the squad found it distracting.

Roper was warming to his theme. "But just because we can't see a reason, doesn't mean there isn't one. In fact, I think that something changed very recently. That would explain why no one seems to be aware of anything: something happened, Sir James reacted, and that's what sealed his death."

Hooley noted he was pacing ever faster and knew this happened when Roper's thoughts were piling up and waiting to be spoken aloud. It was almost as though the man was a production line of ideas.

"At first I thought that they mutilated the body on the spur of the moment. There may have been some sort of confrontation, then his murderers realised they needed to do some clearing up if they were to avoid discovery."

Roper trailed off for a moment, and he stopped pacing.

"I don't want to rule out that it might have been something in his private life, but this feels very controlled and calculated. There was no real effort to hide the body, but removing his head and limbs just made our job a lot harder. Also, the mutilation was done cleanly and efficiently, so it wasn't spontaneous."

Hooley thought that, as usual, Roper had gone to the heart of the matter. He found it fascinating that this was the same man who only yesterday had made such insensitive remarks about his weight, and yet here he was delivering a calm and reasoned analysis.

"Interesting," Hooley said. "I hadn't thought of it that way, but I can see where you're going. Just stick to your instincts on this one. The original detectives did a good job the first time around, and they never found any trace of a secret lover, male or female, so it doesn't appear to be a domestic matter. After his wife died, he apparently withdrew into himself."

Hooley rubbed his hands together, something of a habit. Years ago, Roper had been puzzled by what it meant. Then it dawned on him that after making the gesture, the DCI would leap into action. Roper, who loved cricket with a passion — you could lose yourself in reams of facts — thought it was similar to what was described as a batsman's "trigger movement" as they prepared to play the next ball.

True to form, Hooley stood up suddenly and grabbed his jacket. "Fancy visiting the crime scene, then?" He was already heading towards the door.

Before he could leave, Roper asked, "Can we visit his home first? I think it will help me get more of a feel for the man."

"Fine by me," said Hooley, who looked thoughtful as he stretched his arms wide to make his coat fit comfortably. "Actually, that might be a good idea. Since we confirmed the ID of the body, the warehouse has been awash with people going over every inch of the place. I'm not saying a bad job was done the first time around, but the boss is determined that everything is gone through with a fine-tooth comb.

"They're going back to his house when they finish, either today or tomorrow, so the only company we should have is the poor sod on guard duty at the front door."

He got up and headed for the lift. He didn't look round to see if Roper was following.

7

Sir James Taylor's Eaton Square home was an imposing, five-storey Georgian townhouse, with immaculate white stucco plastered on the front. The black front door was reached by a set of steps. Opposite was the garden area, enclosed by metal railings and usually occupied by uniformed nannies and their young charges. To his complete surprise, Hooley was able to find a parking spot almost outside. He and Roper walked up the short flight of steps to the front door and showed their IDs to the uniformed officer standing by the door.

"Been here long?" said the DCI with sympathy.

"Got here at 5 a.m., sir. It was cold then, but now it's so hot." The sun was beating down on the houses and the PC looked miserable in the full heat of the day.

"Tell you what. If you spot a traffic warden nosing around my car, you have my permission to taser him."

The remark brought a grin, and the constable let them into the house. As the door closed behind them Roper turned to his boss, looking concerned.

"I don't think you should encourage people to go around tasering traffic wardens."

Hooley turned to stare at him. "It was a joke, Jonathan."

"But you told him he had permission to do it. It didn't sound like a joke to me. And you are being very unfair to target people who are only doing their job. Without traffic wardens, the whole city would grind to a halt with drivers just parking where they liked."

The DCI was initially taken aback and then realised that this was precisely the sort of thing over which Roper could become unexpectedly passionate, and decided he needed to sort the issue out straight away.

"The point is, the man is doing a horribly boring job and standing in the sun wearing a heavy uniform. He's obviously fed-up, so I was trying to cheer him up a bit. I can assure you that he won't be shooting anyone."

There was a long pause while this was absorbed.

"I think I understand," said Roper. "You're using distraction theory to create a humorous counterpoint."

Hooley puffed his cheeks out. "I hadn't thought of it quite like that, but I suppose so. Now, shall we get on with what we came for?"

Hooley was silently praying that this would prove a sufficient "distraction" to get them off the topic, and his hopes were answered as Roper went into investigation mode. He reached into his jacket and pulled on a pair of gloves before starting a careful examination of the entranceway.

After watching him for a few moments, Hooley asked, "Are you doing that 3D thing?"

"Yes," said Roper distractedly, who was now fixated on the black-and-white marble floor tiles. He had once told Hooley that he could create a 3D image in his mind of anywhere he visited, if he just took a little time to memorise the details. He said it allowed him to see it from every possible angle. Anyone else and the DCI would have thought this was bollocks, but he knew that if Roper said he could do something, then he could.

Over the next hour, they toured the vast and eerily quiet house. Roper was silent throughout as he maintained concentration and spent a surprising amount of time checking the bathroom. In the master bedroom, he had carefully studied all the suits and clothing hanging in the dressing room. Hooley thought it was especially poignant that despite his wife having been dead for several years, her clothes were still there, carefully preserved in plastic wrapping.

Finishing up on the top floor, Hooley asked him if anything was standing out.

"Not really. I did notice that he had just got a new prescription for his blood pressure medication, so that might suggest he wasn't expecting anything to change in his life. The only thing I don't understand is why he kept his wife's clothes."

"I think he was just holding on to her memory. They were very happy together, by all accounts."

Roper ran his fingers through his hair.

"I don't know why he needed clothes to remember her, not unless his memory was going wrong."

Hooley was grateful that he didn't have to reply to that one, as Roper was off down the stairs.

"I'd like to have another look at his study."

He bounded away, leaving the DCI following and musing on how powerful memories could be.

8

Roper had shot down the stairs, oblivious to the risk of falling. Hooley, following at a more sedate pace, saw him disappear in the direction of the study. A few moments later, the silence was broken by shouting. A jolt of adrenaline helped Hooley overcome his vertigo, and he took the rest of the stairs at a run. Dashing into the room, he expected to find Roper struggling with an intruder. Instead, the younger man was spinning slowly on the spot with his eyes shut. Before he could ask what was going on, the constable guarding the door ran in.

"Is everything OK? I heard shouting and thought you might be in trouble . . ." He trailed off as he took in the gently rotating Roper. "What the . . . ?"

Before he could finish, Hooley calmly gripped his arm and led him out of the room. He gave the man a conspiratorial wink. "Best not to ask."

"But what was he doing? You're not going to tell me that's some sort of new CID thing."

"No, no. It's nothing like that. But I fear the answer may make your head hurt."

The PC quickly went back to his door duty, obviously relieved to leave them to it. Sighing heavily, Hooley made his way back into the study. Roper was waiting for him with an eager expression.

"Could you go into the centre of the room and sing something, or if you can't sing then just shout." Before his fuddled brain could come up with a reply, Roper looked quizzical. "Is that a cross expression on your face?" he asked earnestly.

Hooley rolled his eyes. "Can you explain why you want me to start singing?"

"I want to listen to the echoes. I tried it myself, but my own voice gets stuck in my ears, so it vibrates."

Hooley made a Herculean effort to resist asking what he meant by the sound getting stuck in his ears. He feared the answer might make him feel dizzy. He sighed again and wondered if this was what it was like to find yourself in an alternate reality.

He decided it was best to focus on the room. It was about twenty feet square and maybe fifteen feet high, if he was any judge. There were two large windows on one wall which featured floor-to-ceiling curtains in a thick, lined fabric. They were cream coloured, traced with blue, pink and green flowers. The dominant piece of furniture was an antique desk with a top about six feet wide and almost the same depth. It was polished to such a gleaming golden-brown lustre it was easy to imagine it would be warm to the touch. Behind was a substantial floor-to-ceiling bookcase. Facing the desk were three wall-mounted televisions, and in front of them was a dark green sofa that was almost certainly an original Chesterfield. The carpet was so thick it seemed to deaden all sound.

"You're telling me you can hear echoes in here?" He had a lot of time for Roper, but this was stretching things.

"Of course."

Hooley decided to get it over with. At least no one else was watching.

He strode to where he guessed was the centre, took one final and sceptical look at his colleague and shouted

"ARSENAL!" at the top of his voice. It felt oddly liberating, and he was about to do it again when Roper pointed at the bookcase.

"That's it. There's a space behind that."

Hooley's eyebrows shot up in surprise. "There's a hidden room in here?"

Roper ignored the question as he started searching through the desk drawers. Within a few minutes, he had what looked like two TV remote controls, which he studied carefully, holding them up to take advantage of the light from the windows. He nodded to himself, put one down, and then pointed the other at the bookcase. Nothing happened, then Roper pointed it at a different spot, and to Hooley's astonishment one section silently slid back to reveal a dark opening.

"How did you know that would work?"

Roper held the remote up. "If you look closely, you can see that only the select button has been used. Not the power button." He clicked the remote again, and the door slid shut. Roper pointed at a tiny object on the bookcase. It was so small Hooley had to look closely to see it. "I also noticed this receiver here. It's a line-of-sight system, so you have to point the remote at it to access the room. That's why I couldn't open it the first time. The other one was clearly for the TV because so many buttons have been used." He pointed this one at the three screens, and they all flickered to life.

Hooley shook his head in admiration and looked at both remotes. He couldn't see the difference and would never have spotted the receiver without Roper's help.

He couldn't resist opening and closing the secret door a couple of times before he looked inside. There was a light switch just inside the entrance, and he flicked it on to reveal a space about the size of a large broom cupboard. On one side was a formidable-looking safe and on the other a series of shelves. The only thing on them was a laptop.

He reached in and passed it to Roper, who put it on the desk and flipped it open. After it came to life, he looked at the screen. "Needs a username and password." He passed it back to the DCI and rubbed his temples with his fingertips. "It's interesting about him keeping his wife's clothes. Try her name as the username and let's go for her birthday as the password."

"Well, I know his wife was called Miriam, but I have no idea what her birthday was."

"Tenth of June 1960," said Roper. "So, try 100660."

The combination worked, and Hooley looked at Roper.

"You really are amazing, Jonathan."

"Define amazing — do you mean awesome, surprising, fascinating . . . ?"

Hooley smiled at him. "Just the safe to sort out."

Roper nodded and bent down to grip the dial. "I bet it will be the same as the password." As he spoke, he flicked the dial backwards and forwards and was rewarded as the door came open. To their disappointment, it was empty.

Hooley patted Roper on the back very gently; he knew he disliked too much physical contact. "Let's get back to the office and get stuck into this laptop. He must have had some reason for keeping it well hidden. Is it too much to hope that we might find some leads we can pursue?"

9

Hooley had been surprised when Roper agreed to return to the office without stopping to try and bring the laptop to life. He had expected him to want to dive in without delay, but Roper had already decided it would be best to leave it to the office expert, Gary Malone. "I'm nowhere near his level. He is the obvious person to open it up."

Malone was waiting in Hooley's office when they returned, dressed in his usual T-shirt, jeans and trainers, his long face displaying an expectant expression as they walked in. He greeted Hooley with a respectful "Sir," and Roper with a cheery, "Wotcher mate, long time." The two men got on well. Sometimes they seemed to speak to each other in a short-hand that no one else could follow. The DCI had lost count of the times he had made them repeat something "more slowly and in English, please." The pair sometimes treated him like an ancient relative born in the steam age, but the mild indignity was worth the results.

Malone brandished a tiny flash drive. "I'll copy everything I can on to this first, and then you can look around to your heart's content." He plugged it in, waited briefly, and then keyed in a series of responses.

"That didn't take long," said Roper. "Can't be much in there."

Malone moved his head from side to side, and his bottom lip jutted out. "Not sure yet," he said. "But it's all yours for now. I'll place whatever files I've copied, along with the emails, onto the air-gapped computer. Don't plug that machine into our system until we know there's nothing nasty lurking in the background. Some of these new viruses can disguise themselves pretty effectively, so I need to be very thorough."

Roper watched him hurry away, then sat back and looked expectantly at his boss.

"Where do you want to start?" He waved his hand over the keyboard.

"Check his email for the twenty-fourth of May, the last day anyone saw him." He watched as Roper's nimble fingers flickered into action.

"We've got something." Roper tapped away and produced a list of emails.

"There was an exchange with someone called Oxford52. It started at 11.16 a.m. and finished at 11.21 a.m., so it was over pretty quickly."

Hooley moved behind Roper so he could get a look over his shoulder.

"The first one was sent by Sir James."

JamesTaylor@Miriam.co.uk: I need to speak to you very urgently, and it needs to be in person.
Oxford52@Oxford52.com: Then come along tonight.
JamesTaylor@Miriam.co.uk: I have no interest in the "entertainment" you have planned.
Oxford52@Oxford52.com: I have to be there, then I fly out later tonight. Unless you want to be on the plane, you will have to come.
JamesTaylor@Miriam.co.uk: Under protest, but I will see you there at 9 p.m.

Hooley reread them. "That seems to support your idea that his disappearance was connected to something recent. Is there anything else before that?"

"No," said Roper. "At least not apparently connected to that. There has been some communication with Oxford52, but the previous one was two weeks before and just thanked him for sending over some documents." He stood up. "I think I'd better go and ask Gary about Oxford52 and see if we can discover any more about him."

Twenty minutes later, Roper walked back in to find Julie Mayweather sitting at his desk.

"Brian's just been filling me in on what you've been doing. Fantastic work, Jonathan. Have you been able to get any more information?"

Roper shook his head. "The account for Oxford52 ceased operating the day after Sir James went missing."

"That's your tidying-up theory right there," said Hooley.

Mayweather pushed herself to her feet. She looked at the two men in turn. "Let's try to keep as much of a lid on this as we can. We don't want to alert someone to where we are for the moment. I must report this upwards, so it will end up in political circles, but for now, I will leave out the laptop and the messages. I'll just mention that secret room you found."

As she walked out, Hooley decided he had to find out more about what Roper had done at Eaton Square. It had been bothering him, so he waited for him to sit down. "Would you mind explaining, in simple terms please, how you found that room by getting me to shout?"

Roper shrugged. "I'm not entirely sure, but I think it has something to do with echolocation."

Hooley sat down heavily as he thought about the implications. "You mean like bats do?" There was a long pause while Roper thought about that, then he nodded.

His response brought a rueful grin from Hooley. "I suppose the rest of the team will be calling us the 'Caped Crusaders' from now on."

"What do you mean?" asked Roper.

"You know, Batman and Robin — the Caped Crusaders of Gotham City."

Roper looked blank for a moment — popular TV culture was not one of his strengths — then realisation dawned.

"Does that mean we'll have to start wearing tights and masks?"

Hooley got up and firmly closed the door. Then he stood in front of Roper's desk. "Under no circumstances are you to ever repeat this conversation outside this room."

"But . . ."

Hooley held up a warning finger to silence any more talk.

10

Back in London, as Roper carefully worked his way through the files, Hooley was thinking it was challenging to describe, in conventional terms, how the younger man slotted into a big police team. There was no way he could ever be described as a team player. Especially since some members of the team privately described him as "weird", "spooky" or "rude".

Hooley knew this was unfair. Roper was different, but that was partly because he had such a direct manner, which could see him asking people the most intimate questions without realising he was making them uncomfortable. He could also be abrupt with people who couldn't keep up with the way he approached things. But his motives were always focussed on the investigation and never on his own personal advancement.

The problem was that he could often rub people up the wrong way without even realising it. From simple things like being too engrossed in his work to notice others, to making over-personal comments and looming up behind colleagues and looking at their computer screens. People hated it, but because Roper wasn't concerned if someone did the same to him, it was pretty much impossible to make him understand why colleagues became agitated. That was the thing about him; you got the whole package or nothing at all.

But Hooley knew that as much as some people found Roper difficult, the feeling was reciprocated, and it left the younger man feeling isolated from the rest of the world. The only one he seemed to be comfortable with was Hooley himself. He had once decided to ask him directly why this was; trying to be circumspect with Roper was pointless. Roper listened and then stared at him for a while before he replied, "Your body doesn't shout. Most people are noisy even when they're not talking. And you don't ask silly questions like, 'How are you?'"

Hooley found this fascinating and was reminded of it a couple of weeks later when he had an argument with his wife. She had accused him of being far too passive, and he wondered if this was the effect Roper had been talking about.

He dragged himself out of his reverie. He needed to follow up a call to a friend in HR, to make sure he could see the notes that had been drawn up after Roper had been forced onto the various courses and psychological evaluations.

Not wanting to break strict confidentiality rules, he'd taken the precaution of getting permission from Roper himself, which the younger man had agreed to immediately, telling Hooley, "You need to know everything is OK."

His HR contact said he would have to come into the Scotland Yard building itself, since there was no chance his mate would email copies of confidential documentation. Now he needed to fix a time to do it.

He was looking at his diary when someone walked past the office door carrying a tray of steaming mugs of tea and coffee. The aroma reminded Hooley that he was neglecting his caffeine addiction. Glancing up at the wall clock, he saw it was time for a break and that Roper had been totally immersed in work for nearly two hours. Through trial and error, he had reached the conclusion that this was about as long as he should be left when he was working so intensively.

"Coffee, then an update?" he asked loudly.

Roper looked up, seemingly confused to find himself in an office, and then shook his head before jumping up. "Good idea. I'll go. I like short walks. They help me to think."

With that rapid-fire statement, he was out of the door. Hooley paused in calling out. He actually wanted a tea but then shrugged. Roper was on a mission to get coffee, so the hassle wasn't worth it. They'd end up in a circular discussion about why he had said one thing when he wanted another. That was the kind of conversation he used to have with his wife.

Twenty minutes later, Roper returned armed with drinks and food.

"It's nearly lunchtime," he observed, dumping a smoked salmon sandwich in front of his boss and then producing four chocolate muffins, three of which he lined up on his desk, making sure they were the same distance apart. He waved the extra muffin at Hooley.

"Would you like this?"

Hooley gave him a pointed look. "I think not. After all, you pointed out I was putting on weight."

"Good thinking," said a totally unabashed Roper, and the extra muffin joined the line-up on the desk. "I don't mind eating all of them. I never seem to put on weight, and sugar helps me to concentrate. It seems to work as fuel for my brain."

"Lucky you," said Hooley in a sarcastic tone, which he knew would be wasted on his colleague. He concentrated on his sandwich, aware that Roper had already devoured the first muffin. They ate in silence, and then Hooley took a sip of his coffee. It was still too hot, and he wondered, not for the first time, how some places made coffee so hot it could practically melt the cup, while others made it revoltingly tepid. He blew the surface of his drink to little effect then asked Roper what he had discovered. The younger man blinked rapidly before responding.

"There's not a massive amount of stuff and no apparent 'smoking gun' in there. But he has a fantastic number of personal photographs. Mostly of him and his wife, and it looks like they go right back to before they got married. I've counted 204 pictures so far." He frowned and looked up. "Is that normal?"

41

As far as Hooley knew, Roper only had two photos. One of his parents and one of his grandmother, but nothing from his school or university days. He also shared Hooley's aversion to the idea of selfies.

The DCI took his time responding. He knew this was one of those questions Roper came up with that had an underlying meaning: *Can you help me understand more about people?* After taking another moment, he said, "Well, some people do have happy marriages, you know. Not everyone, I grant you. But in any relationship, there are good and bad bits, and people want to document and remember the good bits." He realised this sounded a bit lame; perhaps he wasn't the best person to ask. He decided to push things on with a question of his own. "Apart from the pictures, is there anything else?"

Roper shook his head. "The only recent stuff — and I'm talking about four weeks before his death — are documents relating to biotech companies looking into cancer treatments and other experimental stuff about extending the human life span."

"You mean living forever?"

"Not forever, but scientists are talking about people routinely living to 150 years old by the end of this century. Although they also say that as we cure current diseases, new ones will emerge. But this stuff seems very cutting edge, at least from what I can make of it."

Hooley rubbed the back of his neck. He could feel the first signs of a headache. Definitely no stopping at the pub tonight.

"I suppose he was always going to follow that sort of path after his wife's death. Have you come across any mention of money?"

"Nothing I've seen so far. But I thought we had all his financial information anyway."

Hooley made a face. "The previous team compiled a lot of information, but it's very complex, and I couldn't begin to tell you if it includes everything he had."

Roper nodded. "I'll keep digging away at what I've found, and Gary can have a look at the emails properly."

The day petered out with a sense of anticlimax. The burst of activity in the morning had promised far more than it eventually delivered, and Hooley decided to call it a day before they both became frustrated. He'd heard the forensic team was almost finished at the warehouse, so he wanted to make an early start.

11

There wasn't much that Dan Sykes was frightened of, especially in people, but he was cautious around Tommy Burton. The man had an extraordinary ability to dig out secrets and then use them to his own advantage. Sykes often wondered how much of his own dirty linen his boss was aware of. He decided it was best to assume he knew it all.

He was mulling this over when his phone rang. It was Burton himself. He had been told the call was coming and wondered if it was going to be bad news. Without being aware that he was doing it, Sykes stood to attention as he grasped the phone.

"Sir."

Never use a name and never say more than you have to. Even if you are using a state-of-the-art phone with regularly updated real-time encryption.

"New man's been brought in. Over to you."

The line went dead.

Sykes looked at the phone. He knew he had just been told to find out everything he could. But it was odd. His boss hadn't seemed especially concerned when the Special Investigations Unit had first got involved. He'd told Sykes it was only to be expected that the Met would assign an elite team once they had confirmation Sir James was dead. In fact, he'd even said he was pleased that the discovery of the body had taken so long, as he had only anticipated a two-week advantage, if they were lucky. The extra time meant they had not just cleared up, they'd even had time to go back and sort out a few niggles. But if Burton was worried about this new player, he was going to have to really get on the case.

He sighed and looked out across the port of Dunkirk in Northern France. He preferred it to Calais or Boulogne-sur-Mer. There was a great little restaurant on the front that did a brilliant *moules-frites*.

Now he was watching one of his men manoeuvre a large suitcase on board. Inside was a young Latvian woman that his team had picked up a few days earlier with the promise of transport to London and a good job. It had been going well, but something had alerted the woman's suspicions as they approached the French coast, so they had been forced to give her a sedative shot to keep her quiet.

The suitcase was placed out of sight in the galley, and within twenty minutes they were underway for Ramsgate in Kent. Sykes could have delegated this job, but every now and then he liked to put in an appearance to keep everyone on their toes. With decent weather, and a steady ten knots, they should make landfall in about five or six hours. He took the view that getting out of the office from time to time stopped him getting stale.

From his position next to the helmsman, he ducked down to talk to the man guarding the suitcase. "As soon as we are out of sight of the coast, you can open it up and let her out." The man nodded to show he'd understood.

An hour later, he was looking out at the English Channel and enjoying the surprisingly warm breeze, when he was disturbed by a shout of "Boss, we got a problem!"

He headed into the cabin to see the young woman laid out of the floor, unmoving. He knew what he was looking at and tapped the body with his foot.

"You've checked its pulse, I take it?"

The man was unconcerned. "Some of them can't handle the tranquilliser."

Sykes said, "I'll give you a hand getting her on deck. We've got some weights up there."

Twenty minutes later the body, now bound in tarpaulin and weighed down, was tossed over the side. *Plenty more fish in the sea*, he thought as the body disappeared. As busy as the English Channel is, it was easy enough to find a quiet spot to dump a body.

Sykes marched to a beat only he could hear. He thought himself a tough and ferocious opponent, but one who had developed what he liked to call his "code of conduct". While he would kill without compunction, the target had to be a player in the game, however tangential the connection might be. The young woman who had just been tossed over the side had deserved to die because she had taken such massive risks. Taking risks was something that Sykes tried to avoid, although he would do it if he thought there was some gain to be had. It explained why he had lasted so long in such a dangerous job. He had been well rewarded for his work in war zones around the world, and over the last ten years he had turned down more offers than he had accepted, such was the demand for men like him.

Those outside his very tight circle could easily be deceived by his appearance. He wasn't physically imposing: he stood about five feet nine inches and was wiry rather than muscular. He was also blessed with a smile, entirely fake, that made most people think he was kind and gentle. But he was far from being a simple thug. He was calculating and had long ago realised he needed more than fighting skills to succeed. This led to him carefully cultivating a team of informants who would, for the right money, find out what he needed to know.

It was this controlled approach that had drawn his latest boss's attention. Burton had approached him one day with an incredible offer. The money was so good he might soon achieve his ambition to run a winery in South America, preferably Chile. But he needed to do his job well and find out who this new player was, pronto. His first move was to contact a man who knew how to navigate his way through the top levels of Scotland Yard. Now he would have to wait for the information to come back. But time was at a premium. He didn't want to be waiting long, or he would be getting another phone call.

12

Roper shivered as he and Hooley walked towards the warehouse. There was a sharp morning chill, but it was claustrophobia that had him pulling his coat tight, triggered by the sense of the enormous buildings pressing down on him. They were in a part of East London that was still waiting for its regeneration boom. The area was home to warehousing once used to store goods that flowed through London's docks. Built in the Victorian era, they were imposing, London-brick constructions. If developers got their way, these would soon be turned into up-market "loft-style" living spaces aimed at the hipsters who had already left their mark in nearby Hoxton. At present, the area was unloved and felt curiously deserted for somewhere so close to the financial centre at Canary Wharf.

It was just after 7 a.m. when they walked up to the building where the body was found. Two white-suited investigators were outside, their faces pinched by the cold.

"Morning boys. Feeling a bit chilly?" Hooley gave them a wide smile.

The older of the two, his bushy eyebrows and glittering eyes giving him a fearsome expression, replied to his bonhomie with a meaningful look.

"It may be summer out here, Chief Inspector Brian Hooley, but it's bloody Arctic in there," he indicated the warehouse with a jerk of his head. "Especially if you've spent the night working hard on behalf of the taxpayer."

Ted Davies was about the same age as Hooley and looked similar, with a round face and an air of broad-shouldered defiance. The pair shook hands, and then Davies introduced his assistant, Tina Morris. She waved in acknowledgement but said nothing. Meanwhile Davies turned his attention to Roper.

"I take it this sharp-eyed young man is your famous assistant, Jonathan Roper?"

Roper froze as he tried to think what was famous about him, only a nudge from Hooley snapping him out of introspection. He realised he was being offered a hand to shake, and he snatched at it before quickly pulling away.

"Any thoughts for us, Ted?" asked Hooley, rolling his eyes in a "What can you do?" gesture at Roper's reaction. The forensic expert shook his head, his face forming into a pantomime of incredulity. Tina tried to hide a smile.

"Now the man expects miracles! We turn up and, just like those rubbish TV shows, someone spots a single human hair from twenty feet away and in one swoop solves the case."

Ted Davies was quite vocal about his disdain for forensic detective shows. Still, his daughter had let slip to colleagues that one of his favourite things was to watch one after the other on TV and shout abuse at the way his profession was portrayed.

"Of course—" a sly expression appeared on his face — "I may have something. Only preliminary observations mind, depends what you have for me."

Hooley held up the small carrier bag he was holding. "Coffee?"

"That'll do nicely."

There was a brief delay while the two CSIs took a few appreciative sips, and then Davies looked more serious.

"Someone's done a pretty decent job of trying to sanitise that warehouse. There's been extensive use of bleach and virtually every surface has been wiped clean, and that must have taken some serious manpower. But, despite all that, we've found traces of blood, so one might suspect that our man was killed and dismembered in the same place he was found. Hopefully, we should be able to confirm that once the results come back.

"There are also a few fingerprints, but don't hold your breath for anything there. I gather the security guard who found the body was blundering around all over the place, so chances are they'll be his."

Hooley nodded. "Thanks for the heads-up. We have the security man on our list of people to talk to. How long before we get the results?"

"That depends on how hard your boss wants to lean on people, but we'll be going as fast as we can."

"Thanks, Ted. OK for us to go in and look around?"

Davies waved his hand at the entrance. "It's all yours. Just remember to suit up first."

He left them to it and walked off with Tina in tow. Donning their gear, Hooley looked at a uniformed policeman standing a few feet away, stamping his feet against the cold. He looked at the entrance and then nodded at Hooley.

Roper, meanwhile, was being driven by a different agenda. "That comment about the 'famous Jonathan Roper' — was that a joke?"

Hooley nodded.

"It was a joke, but not at your expense. That was his way of letting you know he was aware of your talents. So, in a way, it was a compliment."

Roper looked thoughtful but said no more.

* * *

The main door of the warehouse was enormous, the solid dark wood reinforced by metal hinges covered in layer upon layer of black paint. It had originally been designed to allow the passage of horse-drawn carriages. On the right-hand side was a human-sized entrance, through which Hooley stepped into the gloom. Even the powerful array of portable lights set up inside could not reach the furthest spaces, which remained coated in darkness.

"Bit spooky in here," said Hooley. When no reply came, he felt the hairs on the back of his neck stand up. Spinning around, he realised he was entirely alone and hurried back to the entrance. Sticking his head out of the door, he found Roper studying the lock.

As he watched, Roper looked up. "I've found a tiny bit of fresh oil on here. Maybe someone opened the doors recently." He looked for a moment longer, checking in several more spots, and then followed Hooley inside. Roper produced a torch and carefully worked his way around the dark outer reaches. The DCI knew better than to disturb him and left him to it. The slow and careful search took about forty-five minutes. Roper was silent the whole time. Hooley knew he wouldn't speak until he felt he had something to say; there was no time for small talk in Roper's world.

Finally, he seemed satisfied with his examination and gestured towards the shadows. "There's not a lot to see, but I did notice something over there." He walked back to where he had started and tapped his foot on the ground. "I think something heavy may have been here. I can see a sort of square outline." Then he pointed out several other spots where he could also see an outline.

Hooley squinted hard but wasn't sure. "I'll have to take your word for it. I can't really see anything."

Roper nodded thoughtfully. "I expect that's because your eyesight is fading. Another way that age affects you." Hooley practised calm thoughts; it was too early in the morning to worry about Roper insulting his eyesight, and he probably did need a test. "But I think there was a structure here recently. Which is odd, because that security guard told us this has been empty for years."

He watched Roper carefully following a trail only he could see, one that took him straight back outside.

Hooley followed and observed him examining the bottom of the closest lamppost. He appeared to find what he was looking for, as he stood up and nodded then went back inside, calling out, "I'd like to see the basement where the body was found and then come back to have another look up here."

"Fine, go ahead," said Hooley. "I'll follow you down, but first I want to arrange for that security guard to be brought in today. I think he just went up the rankings a little bit. I'm very keen to hear him explain what made him come here on his own and see if he can explain why these doors have been opened recently."

By the time he'd put the request in, Roper was in the basement area where the body had been found. It was worse than the rest of the building. The DCI wouldn't have wanted to come down here without the lights left in place.

Nonetheless, he stuck it out while Roper performed another careful investigation. It was cold down there, and he was glad to climb back up as he finally followed Roper outside, where the younger man started looking up at the other buildings in the area.

"There's no sign of any of these being in use. Do we know if they're owned by the same company?" he asked, gesturing at the warehouse they had just examined.

"No. It's a good question, though. Do you want to head back to Victoria and we can get that in motion?"

As keen as he was to find out what Roper was thinking, he knew that this was one of the times it was best to give him some space to work everything out. He would tell him when he was ready.

An hour later and a uniformed sergeant poked his head around the door of the DCI's office.

"We've got that security guard you wanted, sir. He's parked in the interview room next floor down."

"That's great. How's he behaving?"

"My old mum always told me 'Trevor, never judge a book by its cover.' But, with all due respect, I would say your man is guilty of something. He's as jumpy as the proverbial cat on a hot tin roof. All the way here, he kept wittering on about why we wanted him and how he'd already spoken to the police and didn't know why we wanted to speak to him again. I've left him with a nice cup of tea and told him you'll be with him shortly."

Hooley nodded. "Good to know. I think we'll leave our friend to sweat a little bit more and then see if we can find out what it is that's making him so nervous."

13

Looking through the one-way mirror. Hooley thought George Howard's misery was plain to see, as he kept glancing at the door of the interview room, clearly worried about who was going to walk through it. As Hooley and Roper watched, they saw a bead of sweat trickle down his forehead and into the corner of his right eye.

"He looks a little bit stressed about being here. What do you think, Jonathan?"

"I'd say he was about five feet ten inches, weighs about 175 pounds and does his shopping at Asda."

Hooley turned and stared at him. "OK, Sherlock, the height and weight I might have guessed, but how do you know where he goes shopping?"

Roper didn't say, "Elementary, my dear Hooley," but his expression certainly implied that.

"When he leaned forward just now, I saw the label on his T-shirt. It said 'George', which is the clothing brand label for Asda."

Hooley absorbed this for a moment trying to work out if he was an idiot or was simply in the presence of a superior being. He came to the reluctant conclusion it was both. The only option was to press on.

"OK, when I said, 'What do you think?', I meant what do you think about the look of him? Do you think he appears to be showing signs of stress?"

"I thought you were trying to stop me guessing what's in people's minds."

Hooley silently chastised himself. He had been hoping that with Howard showing such apparent signs of tension, it might be the perfect time for Roper to practise his body language skills. "OK, my mistake. Forget I said that and let's go and talk to him. Let me speak first, and then you jump in if you want."

They opened the door to the interview room, and Howard leapt to his feet. Hooley, who was a little less than six feet, realised that Roper's estimate of his height was spot on, and he was most likely right about his weight. Although only in his twenties, he was already carrying a spare tyre around his middle and showing signs of a double chin. Close up, his hair was greasy.

"Are you arresting me? 'Cos if you are, I want a lawyer."

The words, spoken in a sharp South London accent, tumbled out so fast it was difficult to make out what he was saying.

Hooley decided "good cop" was the best approach — for now.

"Mr Howard, please sit down. Just so we are all clear, you are most certainly not under arrest, there are just a few questions we would like to ask to see if you can clear up a couple of things that are puzzling us."

A look of fear flashed across the man's face, and he sat down heavily on the chair and resumed staring at the floor. Looking at the top of his head, Hooley could see he was already going bald.

"I'm sorry to have to go through this again, but orders from the top and all that." He leaned forward as if he was sharing a confidence. "To be honest, we're under a bit of pressure on this one. Apparently, Sir James had some powerful friends, and they've pulled strings to get us on the case." He looked around pretending to check there was no one eavesdropping. "Apparently, the prime minister is interested."

Howard let out a small sigh. He looked up at Hooley with a pleading expression. "Look, I already told them other blokes."

Hooley was sure the man was hiding something, most probably minor theft. He decided to wait until they confirmed the details from his statement. Then he could ratchet up the pressure.

For the next twenty minutes, he led him through his previous statement, which Howard stuck to without much deviation. Roper sat quietly, listening carefully but saying nothing. It was time to up the tempo.

Hooley raised his voice. "You nicked something, didn't you? Did you take something from the body? That would have been a disgusting thing to do, the state he was in."

Howard looked like he'd been slapped in the face and was gasping for breath. "No, no, no. It was nothin' like that."

"So, what haven't you told us? You do know this is a murder investigation? If you're concealing important evidence, I'll make sure you go down for a very long time. Because it's a murder case, you'd end up in a category A prison with the real hard men. Someone like you is going to have a horrible time."

Howard started shaking violently. "I can't tell you. I can't." He had his head in his hands.

Hooley slammed his hand on the table, speaking very loudly. "Too late for that. Tell me what you're keeping from us. One way or another, you're in big trouble, and you need a friend. Talk to me, and maybe I can help you."

For a long moment, the man sat there holding his head, and then he started talking in a rush like he had when they first came in.

"Two geezers jumped me. They was wearing masks and told me to stay away. They said if they saw me around, they'd shank me. One of 'em stuck the top of 'is knife up me nose and said he'd slice it off, just for starters. Then they gave me a bit of a goin' over — not too bad, just to show they could, I suppose."

Hooley looked at him for a while. He'd bet his pension he was telling the truth.

"So, when did this happen?"

"It was the twenty-fourth of May, me bleedin' birthday. Some present that was."

"Suppose I believe your story. Why on earth did you go back there if they had threatened you?"

"I couldn't stop thinkin' about what they might 'ave been doin'. I thought I'd better 'ave a little look."

Hooley snorted. "Really? You're telling me you're just a concerned citizen, with no ulterior motive?" It was much more likely the guy thought there might be something worth nicking and had gone back to check.

Howard's miserable expression confirmed he'd hit the spot. Hooley looked over at Roper and indicated the door with a nod of his head. Getting up, he said, "You need to stay here for a bit while we decide what to do with you. I'll organise some food and a cup of tea."

Howard said nothing, just returned to staring at the floor.

14

Hooley and Roper were mid-briefing to Mayweather when she had to break off to take a phone call, giving Roper time to study her office. It was more than twice the size of the one he and the DCI were sharing and full of things he found distracting. The walls were covered in pictures and photographs. She had four televisions side-by-side showing national and international news, while underneath them was a table for two printers and a shredder. There was also shelving for books and files, plus a few personal items. The windows were shrouded by thick net curtains and blinds to deter prying eyes.

The room was also big enough to house a small conference table with eight chairs, and on the wall to the right of where Roper sat was a huge, detailed map of London. Glancing down, he looked at the alternating squares of blue and grey carpet tiles, rather than the plain blue that Hooley opted for. To cap it all, there was a steady stream of messengers delivering reports and documents. He was glad he didn't have to spend too much time in there.

She finished the call and switched back to the conversation. "So, what do you want to do with our friend Mr Howard? If nothing else, we could threaten him with a withholding information charge."

"My temptation is to leave that for the moment," said Hooley. "We can always do it later, but if we charge him now he'll clam up, and I'd like to be sure he's told us everything. I suppose the other consideration is, could he be in danger?" He turned to Roper. "Do you have any thoughts on this, Jonathan?"

Roper was quick to dismiss the idea. "I don't think so. He should be quite safe now. He was only in danger at the time they approached him and warned him to stay away. If they thought he was a loose end, they would have come for him after Sir James was killed, but I don't think they were too bothered. He can't identify them properly because of the masks, so why come back for him now? They just wanted him out of the way for a while."

He leaned back, running his fingers through his unruly hair in an attempt to smooth it down. Mayweather watched it spring up defiantly then turned her attention to Hooley. "So, we leave him be for now. It's not as if he can go anywhere. But perhaps get someone else to re-interview him, see if another approach makes a difference. I don't like it when witnesses keep things to themselves."

Hooley was nodding. "Definitely. He's not the sharpest I've spoken to. Maybe get someone else to be his best friend. We were right to think that he was up to something, but need to take stock and decide the best way forward. We've got a lot of people to talk to, and Jonathan wanted to dig around some more on the biotech companies mentioned in the files we found in the laptop."

Mayweather turned her gaze on Roper, whom she knew would be following the conversation closely, even though he appeared to be totally absorbed in a careful study of the carpet. "Do you have any ideas about why he was so interested in that field, Jonathan?"

Roper sat up a bit straighter as he shifted in his seat. He tended to fidget when he didn't have a computer screen to look at. "I just have a lot of questions for now. I was thinking about this last night, and I would really like to know if Sir

James was about to have treatment of some sort. Maybe he'd even started."

Mayweather nodded. "I'm not sure if the new autopsy will show anything, given the state of the body, but perhaps you can talk to his personal doctor. There's a name mentioned in the file."

"It's a funny thing," Hooley interjected. "But there's no one around who was close to him. After his wife died, he focussed on the foundation to the exclusion of everything else. I think that keeping his wife's clothes suggests he either couldn't, or didn't want to, move on."

He glanced at Roper. The idea of a man known by many but having no friends was equally applicable to his younger colleague. Then it struck him that he wasn't so different himself. As he wondered about this, he became aware that his boss was looking at him over the top of her glasses.

"Sorry, ma'am, just got slightly lost in thought for a moment." He rubbed his hands together. "Jonathan and I need to go and do some brainstorming."

He stood up, reflecting on how easy it was to cut yourself off from people. He told himself to make a determined effort to talk to his son and daughter a little more.

15

"I've found something. I think it's going to tell us what happened to Sir James Taylor."

Hooley was utterly taken aback. "I thought you were working on the biotech companies?"

It was just coming up to 6 p.m., and Roper had a slightly glazed look which always appeared when he had been digging hard. "I've been going over our visit to the warehouse," he said, ignoring Hooley's question. "While we were in the meeting with the ADC, I suddenly realised what all those square marks were. They were placements for scaffolding poles used to create some sort of temporary structure, most likely an arena.

"I also noticed that there were drag marks everywhere and that they even went out of the door. When I checked the lamp post outside, I saw that it had been tampered with. An access plate was only partially closed, which would have allowed someone to connect a heavy-duty cable and siphon off a lot of power. The newly oiled hinges provided another clue. Those huge doors must have been opened and closed very recently, which they'd have needed to do to allow them to bring in large items — like the seats and structures for a viewing ring.

"It was while we were talking about the security guard that things started to fall into place. Someone needed him out of the way because there was going to be something there they didn't want him to see. I've watched scaffolders, and they are quick, but judging by the floor markings, they would have needed a couple of days to put up something that big and then take it down."

He stopped and looked at Hooley expectantly. The DCI knew this meant he had more. "Go on, then. Tell me what you've found."

Roper was fully alert. "I've been searching around on the Dark Web and think I've found a video clip. I haven't looked at it yet, but it has the initials JT and the date Sir James went missing."

Hooley's expression went from quizzical to concerned. He knew enough about the lawless space of the Dark Web to understand the implications. "So unless I'm misunderstanding you, there could be something pretty nasty on this clip?"

Roper nodded slowly. "I think there's every chance there will be. The only way to be sure is to look at it. The whole file is about 10 minutes long and looks to be quite high quality."

"Are you sure you're up to this, Jonathan? I can always get someone else to watch it."

"No. I need to do this. But I was hoping we could look at it together."

Hooley got up to close his office door. "We don't want anyone bursting in at the wrong moment." Then he picked up a spare chair and moved over to where he could see Roper's screen. "Ready when you are," he said.

Roper clicked on the clip. At first, it seemed quite normal, but within seconds they were drawn into a nightmare world. The screen showed an arena, forty feet square, surrounded by tiered seating. The ring itself was bordered by four-foot-high linked mesh, and those at ground level would be eyeball level with the action. Hooley feared the worst.

"Is this the warehouse where the body was found?"

Roper nodded. "I think so."

The camera slowly panned around the stands. There must have been dozens of people there, all looking excited and staring at one end of the arena. Suddenly it was clear what they were waiting for. A pair of pit bulls were brought into the ring. Their appearance led to a considerable increase in the volume as people shouted out in excitement. The dogs strained against their leads in their determination to get at each other.

Then the camera zeroed in on the pudgy compère, sweating and red-faced in his too-tight suit, as he bellowed a countdown, and with a huge roar the dogs were released. The fight was over in seconds as one dog grabbed the other by the throat. The camera panned in as a spray of blood splattered over the spectators in the front row. They didn't seem to care. The victorious dog was dragged out by handlers, its powerful jaws still clamped around the neck of the loser. No one tried to take the trophy away.

Hooley shuddered. Not just at the cruelty of the dog fights but also at the pleasure of the audience. Without them wanting to watch, there would have been no fight. He glanced at Roper, who appeared to be coping just fine.

Now the camera was back on the compère. He was telling the audience the next fight was the big one. A very rare competition between two Neapolitan mastiffs flown in from North America earlier that day. He explained that each dog would be paraded separately, followed by a short break to allow the audience to place their bets. When the first dog was brought in, there was total silence. Even through the camera, Hooley could see how big it was. It had thick legs, a huge neck and an enormous head enveloped in loose, wrinkled skin which gave it a menacing, hooded-eye look. It was twice the size of the pit bulls, and its giant paws scattered the liberal quantities of sawdust spread across the floor to soak up the blood.

The camera performed a lingering close-up on a well-dressed woman in the front row, who shrank back as the dog stopped and swung its massive head to make eye contact.

After a long moment, the beast continued on a steady lope around the arena before being led out to be replaced by the second animal, equally fearsome.

At last, both dogs were returned to the arena with two handlers assigned to each one to restrain them. The animals were dragged to opposite sides, all the while keeping their eyes firmly locked onto each other. The compère began a countdown from ten, and by the time he reached halfway, the crowd was on its feet.

Three . . .

Two . . .

One . . .

The handlers unleashed the beasts and vaulted out of the ring. The two dogs charged at each other and met with an audible, meaty thud. They backed off, drool dripping from their open mouths, as they studied each other before advancing again. For such large and brutal-looking dogs, there was a strange delicacy in the way they set off — seeming to move slowly at first, with their muscles rippling under their skin, before clashing in a blur of gaping jaws as each tried to gain the upper hand. This time, one of the dogs managed to tear a lump from the other, making the crowd shout louder than ever. Then both dogs turned their heads to one side at a sudden commotion.

A man — Hooley quickly realised it was Sir James — crashed into the ring, landing heavily on his stomach. Hooley thought he must have been hurled in from just off camera. Sir James lay stunned before fear quickly drove him, scrambling, back to his feet. He tried to get away, but the dogs had him in their sights and charged. As the first grabbed his shoulder and spun him around, the second went for his throat. Sir James's terrified screaming was abruptly cut off as his windpipe was shredded.

"Turn it off, Jonathan," said Hooley. He had gone white. "I need a few minutes before we see any more of that." He pushed himself away from the desk, and the video, taking some deep breaths to combat the rising nausea. It was a few moments before he felt able to turn back to Roper. "So . . . I guess you've found out what happened to him. But why kill him in such a terrible way?"

Roper shook his head slowly. "I don't know. But I was looking at the audience, and they weren't expecting it. They all looked terrified. Maybe it was designed to frighten them too, to make sure they don't talk?"

Hooley looked grim. "Talking of the audience, did the camera capture some of them? We can get stills made and release them to the media, along with that fat little announcer. That should round people up. Get some people talking." He looked over at Roper and was surprised to see a doubtful expression on his face. "But I'm obviously missing something. Tell me what it is."

"I don't think it will be as easy as that," Roper replied, almost apologetically. "I think the only people we see are all minor players who don't know what's happening."

Hooley's hopes faded. He was sure that Roper would be proven right. He made a fist with his right hand and punched his left hand hard as a sign of his exasperation.

16

Dan Sykes was staring at a bacon and egg sandwich. It was made to order: crispy bacon, sliced egg and a touch of mayonnaise served on sliced white bread. It was making his mouth water, and that was the point. Sykes was a firm believer that the more you practised anything, the better you got. So resisting temptation was one of the mental tricks he employed at every opportunity. He thought it kept him sharp and in control.

He was waiting for Tommy Burton to call him. His Scotland Yard contact had come through with the information about the new man on the Special Investigations Unit. He had passed this on to Burton in an email via a secure server a couple of hours ago. Trying to guess how long it would take for a reply was pointless, although he imagined it would be sooner rather than later. But years in the military had induced a powerful sense of fatalism. He was convinced that the moment he took a bite of the food, the phone would ring. He hated being interrupted while eating, so it was an excellent time to practise his self-control and restraint.

Leaning back in his leather-bound office chair, he stared at the sandwich, which he'd placed on a platform constructed from four packs of printer paper. To stop himself from going cross-eyed, he would, from time to time, gaze around the room. His office was on the ground floor of a stupidly expensive house in Mayfair. He'd been told that the desk alone was worth thousands of pounds. It was a retro piece produced by a leading designer. On the wall facing the desk was a five-figure spin painting by a leading British artist. He thought it looked like something a child might produce.

Then there were the windows. Three layers of custom glass, each one toughened to resist bullets. Or at least that was the claim. Over the years he'd developed a healthy scepticism of the latest high-tech kit, much preferring his weaponry to be tried and tested.

He was into the second hour of waiting, quite unbothered by the sandwich becoming cold and congealed. He'd eaten far worse on military missions, deep behind enemy lines. The phone finally burbled into life. He picked up.

Burton spoke immediately.

"I think you should make sure he has something to distract him."

"How much of a distraction are we talking?"

"Nothing broken."

The connection ended.

Sykes picked up his cold sandwich, dropped one half in the bin — mustn't be greedy — and took the first bite. He chewed, swallowed and then put his food down. He didn't like to bolt his meals, it wasn't good for you. Now he looked at the briefing note he'd been sent about Roper. It was quite short, but there was enough information there, including the most important thing of all: his home address. No point trying to get near him while he was at work and surrounded by police officers.

The briefing note made it clear that Roper was a bit of a loose cannon. Something about him almost getting the chop a few months ago. It seemed there were people in the Met who didn't like him and had been disappointed to see him return. His source had also said that these same people insisted any success he had as an investigator owed as much to luck as judgement, since his methods were often impossible to replicate, or even understand. But Sykes wondered about that, especially as it seemed he had a powerful ally in Deputy Assistant Commissioner Julie Mayweather. Another lesson learned long ago: never underestimate an opponent.

He put the note down and shrugged. None of that mattered for now. The important thing was Roper was going to receive a short, sharp lesson. He picked up the photograph that had been sent with the report. He was not impressed by what he saw. In his line of work, forming a serious dislike of a target helped to get the job done. The photo was full length, and Roper was in a dark suit that didn't hide how skinny he was. *You look like a bloody stick insect in a suit*, Sykes thought to himself. Then he looked at the hair, all curly and sticking up. If there was one thing Sykes hated, it was scruffy hair.

He wondered about doing the job himself. It would get him out for a bit, but he knew Burton would go mad if he didn't delegate the real grunt work. He was going to have to pass this one on — Pat was the man. He never lost his cool and was good at administering beatings without them going wrong. Pat enjoyed his work; it was why Sykes used him. He always thought those who brought a little passion to the game were the best operators. He shook his head. He would take enthusiasm over ambition any time. Too many people were in it for the money. Soft bastards. They always ran when it got difficult.

He decided that once he'd briefed Pat, he would get out for a while. There were a couple of sites he needed to visit. Make sure that things were going smoothly. They'd been operating at full capacity for six months now, and so far, nothing had gone wrong. He knew from experience that it couldn't last, but being careful would keep that clean record going as long as possible. And at least he would be doing something, rather than waiting and watching all the time. He smiled as another thought hit him. The last shipment of women had been here for a few days now and would have been cleaned up nicely, ready for him to exercise his right as boss to the "perks".

17

"You OK, Jonathan?" The younger man was staring into space. No response. He tried again. "I said, are you there, mate?"

Still nothing. Now he was in a dilemma. Should he interrupt him or not? He decided to leave it a bit longer and was rewarded when Roper suddenly sat up, blinking rapidly.

"Did you just say something, Brian?" he asked.

"I was just checking everything was alright."

Roper gave him a puzzled look. "Why would you do that?"

"I spoke to you twice, and you didn't respond."

Roper nodded slowly. "That's because I was trying something out in my head. I think it might help us with the case. It's a different way of sorting out all the information we have."

Hooley's eyebrows rose as he wondered whether to ask or just wait for an answer. Roper saved him the worry.

"I haven't quite got it right yet. I'm going to need to work on it a little more." Then a huge smile lit up his face; it made him look like a young boy. "But I think it could be very good. It's already helped me remember the name and telephone number of his personal doctor."

Hooley looked at the pile of documents on his desk, just part of what had been generated by two investigative teams.

These were the ones that he had printed out, there was plenty more online. He pointed at the files. "I know you've got a memory like an elephant, but surely extracting something from this lot is difficult?"

"Yes," said Roper. "Under the old way of thinking, it would be. I'd have got there in the end, but this allows me to remember things much more easily." He leaned forward, his enthusiasm evident. "Actually, I could show you some of it now. It's quite easy, really. All you have to do is . . ."

Hooley jumped in before he was given a detailed explanation. "Don't worry. I'll take your word for it. I'm not sure my little grey cells are up to new tricks at the moment. I take it you intend to call this doctor and see if he can tell us about Sir James. Give it a go, but remember that doctors can get hung up on confidentiality, even when we're talking about someone who's died."

Roper made the call, only to be told that Dr Paul Humbert would have to call him back. His secretary said he might be able to ring around mid-afternoon. No longer distracted by his attempt to speak to the doctor, Roper realised it was already 1.30 p.m. and asked Hooley if he wanted something to eat.

"I'll go," said the DCI. "I've decided that I need to start eating a bit more salad and a bit less bread, so I want to see what my options are."

"Sprouting crimson lentils," said Roper.

Hooley looked at Roper as if he had just "sprouted" a pair of horns. "Sorry, what did you say?"

"I said sprouting crimson lentils. Very good for you, especially in a salad. Some people call it a super-food, although that's not true, but it does fill you up. You should also try a kale smoothie, full of vitamins and minerals."

Hooley sighed heavily. "Thanks for the motivational chat. I can't wait to try it. The kale smoothie sounds a particularly horrid invention. I'll bet that becomes a real favourite of mine." He brightened up as a thought hit him. "What about those root vegetable crisps? Those must be good for you."

"No. Full of fat. You'll never get rid of that stomach if you eat things like that, and think what the salt will do to your blood pressure."

The DCI restrained an impulse to flip the finger and took a calming breath, something he was getting plenty of practice at. "Well, I'm going out to get something. What can I get for you?"

Roper rubbed his hands eagerly.

"I'd like one egg mayo on brown bread, a prawn mayonnaise on brown bread, one chocolate muffin and one blueberry muffin. Actually, make that one chocolate muffin and two blueberry muffins."

Hooley stood up, shaking his head. "Anything else?"

"They do a really good vanilla milkshake with organic ice cream, but I'll go and get one of those later. Be good to stretch my legs a bit."

* * *

Roper put the phone down. Dr Humbert had been polite and answered his questions, but it hadn't added anything to the investigation. Hooley looked over. "Any use?"

"He said there was nothing about Sir James's health that warranted any treatment, and he was in excellent shape."

"Shame," said Hooley. "It would've been nice if there'd been something we could look into. Still, at least now you can focus on drawing up a plan for talking to the biotech firms."

Roper nodded. "I've started researching what they do. I'll be ready by tomorrow."

They sat in silence for a minute, then Hooley stood up.

"Come on. We've had a long day. Let's get off home then start early tomorrow." Looking out of the window, he noticed the sun was shining. "Seems quite nice out there. Why don't you walk home? You always say that walking lets you think about things."

18

Roper had pushed himself hard on his walk and was breathing heavily as the entrance to his block came into view. He slowed down and was just imagining the sensation of stepping under a hot shower when he was struck on the back of his head by a fierce blow. Before he could react, a second one hit him, and then strong hands grabbed him, throwing him to the pavement. Already winded, hitting the ground left him stunned, and he didn't move as a hard kick to his stomach was followed by blows raining down on his face, body and legs. Then it was over as quickly as it had started. He threw up violently before blacking out, blood pouring from a cut to his head.

When he came to, he was lying in a strange bed and felt as though he was floating. The light was harsh, and everything seemed white. Part of his mind wondered if he was dead. Gradually the room came into view along with the faces of Julie Mayweather and Brian Hooley. Unless they had died too, it was unlikely they were all in the afterlife. He tried to struggle up, but a gentle hand from Mayweather pushed him back onto the hospital bed.

"You've been hurt, Jonathan, but it's going to be OK. The doctors are coming to look at you again, but you're a tough old bugger."

He tried to speak, but his lips stuck together. Just at that moment, a male nurse loomed into view and gently wiped his mouth with a damp cloth. It let him part his lips, and he tried again to sit up, but this time the room spun, and he sank back without anyone needing to stop him.

"Steady there," said the nurse. "You've been in the wars. The doctor hadn't expected to see you come around quite so soon."

Two minutes later, a tired-looking man walked in and stood at the end of the bed, studying Roper.

"My name's Leo Gu," he said. "I'm an A&E consultant here at Guy's. We've got you in one of our side rooms for the moment, but we'll move you up to a ward as soon as we're happy that you're in a nice stable condition."

He carried on looking at him and then checked the monitors he was attached to.

"That's good," he pointed at one of the displays. "When you came in here, your blood pressure was spiking a bit, but you're already heading back down to normal. You must be fit. That's good. I just need to have a quick look, and then we can think about moving you."

With that, he carried out a slow examination, including shining a torch into his eyes. He nodded, seemingly pleased by what he saw. Then he held up three fingers.

"Not the most scientific of tests, but sometimes the old techniques work best. Could you tell me how many fingers I'm holding up?"

"Three," croaked Roper.

"Good." He held up a single finger. "How many now?"

"One," although it came out sounding like "on".

"Excellent," the consultant smiled at him. "We'll keep an eye on you for a bit longer, but I think everything is going to be fine."

He turned to Mayweather and Hooley and indicated they follow him through the curtains.

"Is he really going to be OK?" said an anxious Hooley as they stepped outside. Before the consultant could reply, they had to step back as an ambulance crew wheeled a trolley past with a pale-looking old lady sucking oxygen from a mask, followed by an orderly pushing a chair with a young boy sporting an enormous bandage on his head.

The consultant shrugged. "Good job it's not Friday or Saturday night. Can be a bit chaotic in here. But you want to know about your man. I do think he'll be fine. In a way, this is one of the more unusual things I've seen. When the ambulance brought him in, he was unconscious and covered in blood. A lot of that was from a head wound, and they can bleed for Britain.

"At first, I thought he must have been hit by a car, even a bus, but the more I examined him, the odder it was. He's been beaten all over his body and head. But nothing seems to be broken, and there don't appear to be any internal injuries, apart from some nasty bruising. He also has a minor concussion. Still, the signs are reasonably hopeful. Time will tell, of course. We haven't been able to get him in for a CAT scan yet, but he's passed the initial checks.

"We need to check his kidney function, but with luck he'll be out of here in a couple of days, three at the most. As I say, quite remarkable."

The two officers watched him walk away.

Hooley spoke first. "Am I the only one thinking he was beaten by a professional who knew exactly what he was doing?"

Mayweather's expression was grave. "You're not. But I also think we need to be very careful before we jump to conclusions. Over the years, how many odd things have we seen? People killed with one punch while someone else gets run over and walks away with just scratches."

She stopped talking, and a more troubled expression crossed her face. Hooley recognised it for what it was.

"You're worried he might have got himself tangled up in something. Well, the good news is that all we need to do is ask him. He's quite incapable of telling a lie."

Mayweather looked dubious.

"No, really," said Hooley. "It's classic Roper. When he was a boy, his grandmother told him that he should never tell a lie because his nose would grow bigger, like Pinocchio. He was so worried about it he never has."

Mayweather was smiling now, the first time she'd relaxed since hearing the news about Roper. "Yeah, I guess that's exactly what our man is like. Once a promise is given, it can never be broken." She thought for a moment. "How do you think he's going to cope with it, though?"

Hooley looked at the curtain closing off the cubicle. "I really don't know. Tell you what, why don't I stay with him until they take him up to the ward? You're going to have a lot of people to talk to about this. I'll let you know how he is and then check on him first thing in the morning. I'd normally leave that to his family or friends, but we're it, basically."

"OK. In the meantime, I'll arrange for a police guard. If in doubt, plan for the worst. Then I'll need to talk to the commissioner."

Hooley watched Mayweather make her way out of the hospital, then pushed his way back through the curtain.

* * *

An hour later, Hooley, who had somehow managed to fall asleep on an uncomfortable chair, was woken by a gentle prod. He opened his eyes and saw the consultant.

"We're just going to take him up to the ward, Chief Inspector. And there's a huge policeman outside who says he'll make sure Mr Roper stays safe. My advice to you is to get home and into bed. He's fine now, so you can relax."

Hooley stood up gingerly. Judging by the protest coming from his back, he was going to regret nodding off. He stepped outside and was immediately impressed by the guard his boss had arranged. The uniformed PC was seriously large and had the sort of forbidding expression that would make most people think twice.

He nodded at the policeman and set off for the exit.

"Good night, sir. I'll keep an eye on him," the officer said as he walked past.

19

The enormous policeman was grinning broadly as Hooley endured a grilling from the sister in charge. The DCI had come back to the hospital just after 6 a.m. and made his way up to the ward, where he found the officer still looking as fresh as he had the previous evening. He had been about to speak to him when he was stopped in his tracks by the nurse.

"I presume you're yet another police officer. It's bad enough that we had that big lump hanging around all night. I take it you've heard of visiting hours?"

He opened his mouth to respond, but she continued before he could get a word in.

"The patients in here are my responsibility, and what Mr Roper needs now is rest, not lots of people disturbing him."

He noticed that he was getting amused looks from two other nursing staff who were busy on their morning round. He held his hands up in what he hoped was a suitably placatory gesture.

"I know it's very early, but Jonathan isn't just a victim here, he's a witness. We haven't been able to establish exactly what happened, and the more information we can get, and the sooner we do it, the better chance we have of catching whoever did this."

"Humph." The woman's expression said she seriously doubted that. "Well, you're going to have to wait. We're just doing the morning checks, and he's due his latest medication, so it will be another ten minutes yet."

With that, she was off. Despite the telling-off, he couldn't help think that in other circumstances he would have found her quite attractive. She was about forty, slim, with short black hair. But there was a look in her eye that made him realise she was not to be trifled with. He decided to keep his head down and talk to the officer.

"Have you been put through the wringer as well?"

"Only a bit, sir. She turned up about an hour ago. Told me off and then went to see her patients. I gather your bloke is doing OK. The night nurse kept me informed. I stayed here, but they've got him in a room down there," he pointed to the far end of the ward. "This is the only way in, so it seemed the best option." He looked over Hooley's shoulder and smiled. "I think that's my relief. I'll be off, and I hope you get whoever did it."

The DCI was just starting to talk to the new arrival when the sister returned. "You can go in now. But no longer than ten minutes, and I'm keeping an eye on the clock," she said, with a meaningful look.

Hooley made his escape and went off to find Roper, who, all things considered, was looking reasonably well. He was sitting up in bed wearing a hospital gown and gingerly sipping a glass of water. His left temple was a livid red, and there were red marks on his left arm.

"I ache everywhere," he announced.

"I'm not surprised. It seems you took quite a thumping. Can you remember anything about it?"

Roper went to shake his head and then groaned, clearly thinking better of it. "Not really. I was about to walk into my building when I was hit from behind, after that it's a bit of a blur. I can remember being hit a few more times, and then the next thing I knew I was in this room. Were you and Julie here at some point, or did I dream that?"

Hooley watched the younger man gingerly flex his left arm before replying. "Yes, but not in this room. We saw you in A&E last night, about 8 p.m. You did wake up for a bit, but that was it. Once the doctor said you were going to be OK, we left you to it."

A worried expression appeared on Roper's face. "How did I get to the hospital? I don't remember that at all."

"Someone saw you being attacked and called 999. When the hospital people found your ID, they called us. Apparently, you were drifting in and out of consciousness. We've got a vague description of a man, shorter than you, wearing jeans and a leather jacket. But the witness said it all happened so fast they couldn't quite work out what they were looking at. The witness also said the attacker ran off towards the river. We'll have people there tonight, see if we can find anyone else who saw something, and we'll be trawling CCTV."

Hooley hesitated over asking the next question, he didn't want to push him too soon, but the need to know won out. "I'm sorry to ask this, but have you been in an argument with anyone recently? Anything at all, no matter how minor?"

Roper shook his head, then winced and gave Hooley a weak smile. "I need to keep my head still. But to answer your question, no, nothing like that. The truth is that until I came back to work, I hadn't really spoken to anyone at all. In fact, I've only spoken to you and the ADC in that time. And the support group, of course, but I didn't get to know any of them. Not like you and Julie. Why? Do you think it might have been someone I know?"

Now it was Hooley's turn to shake his head. "I just wanted to be certain and ask straight away. But my gut instinct is that it won't be anyone you know. I also doubt it was a mugging — otherwise, you would have lost your wallet and phone."

Roper grimaced as he tried to gingerly haul himself into a more comfortable position. "So, what was the reason, then?"

Hooley took a deep breath. "I think we have to consider that what triggered this was you finding that secret room. If the people who killed Sir James are willing to mutilate his corpse to cover their tracks, then why not attack an investigator?"

Roper closed his eyes and leaned back against his pillows. "Yes. I can see the logic." He opened his eyes again and glanced at the DCI. "Thinking about my wallet, do you know where it is?"

Hooley reached into his jacket. "Sorry, Jonathan, I'd forget my own head if it wasn't attached to me. I took it and your phone home for safekeeping. I've got them with me." He reached into his inside jacket pocket.

Roper managed to gesture at the side table unit. "There's a drawer in there you can put them in."

"Again, just for the record, can you check your wallet to make sure nothing's been taken?"

He opened it carefully and held it so Roper could see. "All my cards are present, and I can see the money I had in there."

At that point, the sister appeared in the doorway. It was time to go, and she was pointing at the exit to make the point.

"I'll be back later. You keep taking the pills." He stopped in the doorway. "We'll get you out of here as soon as possible. My granny always used to say, 'The best way to keep well is to stay out of hospital.'" He cast a nervous glance at the fearsome sister, but if she'd heard, she hadn't reacted.

20

Hooley had a plan and was trying to convince his boss. "I think he should stay with me once he gets out. He hasn't got anyone else to keep an eye on him."

Sitting behind her desk with her arms folded, Mayweather clearly had her doubts and had yet to ask him to sit down. "Don't you think it will get a bit much? You've already got him camping in your office, and now you'll have no escape."

Hooley laughed. "He's not that bad. Most of the time, he hardly says a word. Then we have short bursts of conversation I can't quite understand, followed by even shorter bursts of things I do understand.

"I think the biggest problem is making sure I have enough food in. The last time I saw anyone packing it away like that was when my son was little. He was always emptying the fridge. It used to get him a right earful from his mother because he never told her when he'd finished something off."

Mayweather smiled. "I've only got to look at food to put on weight, but he just eats what he likes. If someone could bottle him, they'd make a fortune in the diet business." She looked over the top of her glasses. "I agree he'll need someone to keep watch over him once he gets out. I could fix for a family liaison officer to stay with him."

"Not a chance," said Hooley. "There's no way he could cope with someone he didn't know hanging around."

"Well, so long as you're comfortable with this, then go ahead." Mayweather waved at the chair in front of her desk. "In the meantime, we have the small matter of an investigation to run."

She was a "light touch" boss, happy to allow Hooley the freedom to run the details but always insisting on being kept in the loop. They worked well together, and Hooley knew he was lucky to have her as his boss.

"We've fixed to talk to the housekeeper and the driver later today. I was going to take Jonathan with me, so now I need to take someone else. I don't know if you want to sit in?"

She grimaced. "Actually, I'd love to. But one of us needs to go to a briefing with the forensic accountants. They want to give us an update on what they've found in Sir James's affairs. I gather it's all pretty technical, but it needs to be done."

"Do I need to come along?" said Hooley, barely masking his lack of enthusiasm.

She shook her head. "No need to worry. I know you hate that kind of thing. Anyway, there is one advantage of rank. I can listen politely while most of it goes over my head, and then insist on a detailed report with the all-important 'idiot's guide' — or summary, as they like to call it."

"Very wise, ma'am, very wise." Hooley checked his watch. "If you don't mind, I want to put a call in to the forensic team."

As he walked back into his office, he looked over at Roper's desk. Although he'd only been sitting there for a couple of days, it seemed strange not to have him around, glued to his computer screen and demolishing whatever food was to hand.

Given how much progress they'd already made, thanks to Roper's astonishing insights, he knew he was going to have to resist the temptation to rush him back — or allow

Jonathan to rush himself back. That would be much easier said than done.

He called forensics and learned he would have to wait until tomorrow. He could come in or they would email the details. He hated the mortuary, so if there was a chance of avoiding it, then he'd take it.

21

Hooley was trying to look casual as he made his way towards Roper's room, but he couldn't help walking on tiptoes as he thought about the ward sister. He froze as he heard her speaking from right behind him. Damn, the woman was as light on her feet as Mayweather.

"Good of you to appear at official visiting times." She had one eyebrow raised and was looking at him with an expression he couldn't quite read.

"Hello again, sister," he said with forced joviality. "I must say you've put in a long day. It's nearly eight o'clock."

"Well, you're not doing too shabbily yourself on that front." Her eyes flicked up and down as she checked his appearance, leaving Hooley hoping he hadn't got stains on his clothes.

"Your Mr Roper tells me you're a detective chief inspector. I suppose that's quite impressive."

Then she turned on her heel. To his surprise, he was sweating. Had she just been flirting with him? After thirty years of marriage, he had no point of reference. His mouth felt dry, and he looked around for a water fountain. Feeling more composed after a drink, he set off to see Roper. Walking into the room he thought he looked brighter, although it was clear he was going to have some cracking bruises emerging over the next few days.

Roper was staring at his phone but looked up as he heard Hooley walk in.

"I knew you were close by," said Roper.

"Really?"

"Yes. Hush Puppies sound very distinctive, especially on the type of flooring they use in hospitals. Leather-soled shoes sound quite different."

Despite himself, Hooley was fascinated. "Can you tell who anyone is by the sound of their shoes?"

"So long as I've heard them walking before. Even if people are wearing the same type of shoes, everyone walks slightly differently. Some people sort of scuff their feet, some favour one foot and others march about. You're a marcher."

Hooley was surprised at how pleased he was by this. He'd have been disappointed if he'd turned out to be a scuffler.

Roper clearly wanted to talk some more, and since Roper had raised the topic, he decided to ask him more about his acute sense of hearing. He still hadn't gotten over his surprise at Roper discovering the hidden room.

"Have you always had very good hearing or is it something you had to teach yourself?"

Roper shifted in his bed. He looked far more comfortable than this morning. "I've never really thought about it. When I lived with my grandmother in Kent, her house backed onto the track for the Romney, Hythe and Dymchurch light railway. When the trains approached a crossing about half-a-mile from her house, they whistled to warn motorists. I could always tell which whistle belonged to which engine, even though I couldn't see it."

Hooley shook his head and grinned. "I'm quite keen on steam trains myself, but I hadn't realised that all steam whistles sound different."

Roper shrugged. "If you think about it, they're hand-made, so it's obvious they'll make different sounds."

"Well, it may be obvious to you, but I'm not sure I'd be able to tell the difference. In fact, I know I wouldn't. Anyway, how are you feeling now, and what do the doctors say?"

Roper shuffled up against the pillows.

"Very sore, but it has given me a chance to practice using meditation techniques to relieve pain. It's been working well, and I haven't had any drugs since this morning. The consultant was here an hour ago and said I was making good progress, although I do have a mild concussion. If I have a good night, they might send me home after rounds tomorrow."

Hooley nodded and sat down on the chair next to the bed. What he said next might sound better if he made out it was Mayweather's idea.

"Now, about going home. Julie and I were talking about you, and she feels it might be better if you were with someone for a couple of days. Especially if we're talking about concussion."

Roper looked doubtful. "I haven't got anyone that could come and stay with me."

"Yes, we realised that, so why don't you stay with me for a couple of days? Just to make sure you're making a good recovery, then you can go back home."

He waited while Roper thought about this.

"Actually, that is a good idea."

Hooley covered his surprise. He had been anticipating more of a discussion.

Roper carried on. "Have you spoken to your wife about me staying? Is she happy?"

"Ah well, the thing is, we're having what you might call a trial separation."

"A trial separation?"

"She kicked me out, more to the point."

Roper was clearly about to launch into a series of questions. Hooley held his hands up, palm outwards.

"To be honest, I'm not sure I quite understand it myself, and I don't really want to talk about it. The point is, my brother Tony is a property developer and quite a good one; he's lent me a two-bedroomed flat in Pimlico. It's one of those big old Georgian buildings, so you'd have your own bedroom and bathroom. There's plenty of space, so we wouldn't get on top of each other."

Roper thought for a moment. "Is this also something to do with me being attacked? Do you think it might happen again?"

Hooley shrugged. "We don't know. Until we do, it doesn't hurt to take a few precautions. If it is connected to the case, then I take that to be a positive thing in the sense that we, or you, must be doing something right. At the same time, I would always prefer to be careful."

Roper shifted around in the bed, then asked if there had been any developments while he was in the hospital.

"Well, nothing yet, but you've only been here for a day. We should get the new analysis of what they found in the warehouse tomorrow. I spent most of today talking to the housekeeper and driver, but they haven't added anything new. I think they're quite genuine; they were both very distressed that Sir James was dead."

He noticed that Roper was starting to look tired and decided to leave him to rest. He stood up.

"If they do let you out tomorrow, call me and we can arrange for the policeman on duty here to take you home and get some stuff. I'm assuming that with your iris recognition system only you can get through the door. Make sure you get everything you need for about a week. I'll come down to Pimlico to let you in."

22

Hooley was carefully shifting piles of documentation as he searched for his phone. He knew it was hidden somewhere on his desk, he'd just heard it ping to announce an incoming email. After a laborious morning spent ploughing through details of Sir James's financial affairs, he was desperate to find something to distract him. That email might be just the ticket, if only he could find his mobile.

Finally locating it, he saw that the message was from the Home Office pathologist, Kirsty Goodchild. She oversaw the lab and always took an interest in the most significant cases. He was delighted to read that she wanted to talk to him urgently, just the excuse he needed to abandon what he was doing. He decided to call her without reading any of the attached files. They'd worked together long enough to know that he preferred a verbal heads-up before the written details.

The pathologist answered on the third ring. He knew that if she didn't respond by then, she was carrying out an autopsy. Goodchild brushed aside his attempts to apologise for not looking at her report. "No worries, DCI Hooley. I'd much rather talk to you, anyway. At least I know you pay attention to what I tell you."

"Thanks, doc." One of the reasons they got on was because she shared a similar outlook, which meant he could dive in straight away. "Am I right in hoping that you have something interesting for me?" Despite his best efforts, he couldn't keep the eagerness out of his voice.

She laughed again. "You are, but I'm not entirely sure what you'll make of it."

Hooley sat a little straighter in his chair. It looked like this case was going to bring one surprise after another. "OK, try me."

"For the second sweep of the warehouse, I widened the search area, and we found a new blood trace about ten feet from the original site. It was animal blood. I've spoken to colleagues at the Royal Veterinary College, and they should be getting back to me soon to tell me if they can identify what kind of animal it was from."

Hooley was glad that she couldn't see his face, as he had gone red with embarrassment that he hadn't got around to telling her lab about the video file that Roper had discovered. He tried to find a way out and realised he just had to front up.

"Actually, I owe you an apology. Jonathan found a video on the Dark Web. It shows someone holding a series of dog-fights at the warehouse, and Sir James was killed when he was tossed into a cage with a couple of monster dogs."

He braced for a justified bollocking, but she surprised him by staying calm. "I have to admit that's pretty good. Quite a variation on the 'dog ate my homework' excuse. Anyway, that fits with another finding. There's one area on the ground floor which is saturated in Sir James's blood, and that's most likely the spot where he bled out. Your information also confirms that he was dead before he was chopped up.

"From my findings, I also agree that whoever made the cuts to his head, arms and legs knew what they were doing. The cuts were exact and expert. While I'm not saying it was a surgeon, they were clean and not the sort of thing that would be done by an amateur. That would suggest someone like an abattoir worker or a butcher."

Hooley shook his head. Gruesome as it was, this was the detail that backed up Roper's theory. He ended the call and decided fresh air and a coffee run would do him good. A short while later, he was sitting at his desk with his Americano. He stretched to pick up a file and winced at a sudden pain in his back. It felt like he had pulled a muscle. He rubbed at the spot, wishing he hadn't fallen asleep at the hospital. Opening his desk drawer, he searched around to find some painkillers. Faced with hot coffee or cold tea to wash them down, he grimaced and chose the tea. The pills were just starting to take the edge off the pain when Julie Mayweather walked in with a face like thunder.

"Exciting morning with the commissioner?" he asked, keeping a straight face. He knew that look.

"That man can be bloody patronising. When I told him about Roper being attacked and our worries that it was connected to the murder, he as good as laughed at me. I was reminded that I needed to stay 'objective' and 'not let my emotions get in the way'." She shook her head angrily. "I bet he wouldn't have said that to a man, but he feels he can get away with it with me. I nearly lost my temper, but fortunately, Hugh Robertson was there and stepped in before I could say anything. So now the 'official' line is that Jonathan was the victim of a random mugging."

Mayweather took a deep breath, making a determined effort to get her temper back under control. She looked around and sat on the edge of Roper's desk. "The commissioner had his new PR man there again. He's nearly as bad as the commissioner. When I showed them that video Jonathan found, the fool told me we had to be careful how we used it. What does he think we're going to do, upload it to YouTube?"

She picked up the *Evening Standard*, which was carrying a carefully selected range of mug shots lifted from the video clip. The paper had not been informed that they were taken from a film that showed Sir James's death, just that they were potential witnesses who were among the last to see him alive. If the paper ever found out, there would likely be complaints. Still, she calculated it was a risk that had to be taken to avoid causing a media frenzy.

Holding the paper up so that Hooley could see it, she said, "Any joy in finding out who these people are?"

Hooley shook his head.

Mayweather picked up a scrap of paper and savagely crushed it in her hand. It was clearly going to take more than deep breathing to calm her down. She made to leave the office. "Give me five minutes and then come in. I want to go through all the details with you. I just need to stick a few pins in my commissioner doll."

23

"They're letting me go home, and I can get back to work tomorrow." Roper had called Hooley at lunchtime. He said his police guard was going to run him home then take him to Pimlico. "When we get to my flat, I'm going to treat myself to a long, hot shower followed by one of my special teas."

Roper had once read that strong sweet tea was a natural remedy for shock. He had tried it out and found it effective, so now he seized on any opportunity to drink it. Hooley shuddered as he recalled his one experience of this so-called miracle cure. Roper had made him a cup when he was suffering the lingering after-effects of a heavy cold. He'd presented the drink with great ceremony and was visibly disappointed when Hooley spat out his first sip. It was so sweet it made his mouth dry and his teeth ache. He'd been surprised it hadn't induced instant diabetes.

He swapped his phone from his right hand to his left. "Apart from the tea, I'm delighted to hear you're being allowed home. Take your time, then call me when you're ready to leave your place for the journey to mine. It takes me fifteen minutes to walk back to Pimlico, so if we leave at the same time, I will get there ahead of you. Don't forget to bring clothes."

He put the phone down and smiled as he imagined the look on the PC's face when he saw how many suits, shirts, ties and shoes that Roper was likely to bring with him. To those who like to say death and taxes were the two great certainties, you could add a third: Roper would appear every day in a freshly laundered version of his work outfit. He walked into Mayweather's office to share the news about Roper being sent home, only to find her staring in disgust at her computer terminal.

"The HR department has come up with another brilliant initiative."

Hooley lowered himself into his seat and waited.

"This time they're asking me to get all the members of the unit to contribute their thoughts towards establishing new guidelines on, and I quote, 'The challenges faced in policing London in the digital age.'"

Hooley nodded gravely. "Almost philosophical for them."

"Ha." Mayweather snorted. "I think the best thing to do is ignore it. If I start asking people for their views about theoretical policing when they're already carrying huge workloads, I'll have a riot on my hands. I bet this was dreamed up by the commissioner's new PR team."

Hooley nodded. "They're claiming their ideas will make sure the commissioner avoids any more scrapes with politicians or journalists. Well, all I can say is good luck with that. Some of our colleagues are already muttering about 'Facebook Plod'." He rubbed at his temples, then straightened up in his chair. "Back in the real world, we have some good news. Jonathan has been discharged and is going home to get cleaned up. He should be at mine in a few hours."

Mayweather clapped her hands. "That is good news. With a head injury you can never be sure. He's done well to get back on his feet."

"Amen to that," said Hooley. "I'm trying not to push him too hard, but knowing him, the problem will be stopping him working. Now, on the investigation front, we're still ploughing through all the people who need re-interviewing, and I'd like to put the security guard on police bail. We could charge him, but I'm not sure what it would achieve. He's just a prat who's managed to get himself involved in a major murder investigation through his own bad luck. So far, the press hasn't cottoned on to him, and I think it might be better that way. We'll just warn him that if anyone approaches him, he keeps quiet or he'll be in big trouble."

She nodded in agreement. "Good idea. We don't need him side-tracking us. Is there anything else we need to talk about now?"

"Just the one thing," said Hooley. "Assuming Jonathan is at work tomorrow, I want him back on those biotech companies. He clearly thinks they're going to be important. The other priority, as I see things, is finding out who attacked him. It seems pretty obvious it's related to the investigation."

"You won't find any disagreement from me," said Mayweather, pushing her glasses back up her nose. "If he was targeted in the way we think, that creates another worry. He'd only been back with us for a few days, so it would suggest someone has a direct line into us." She paused for a moment and pursed her lips. "The worst thing about these situations is that you start to doubt the people around you. I keep wondering about the commissioner and his team. Apart from us, they were the only ones who knew that he'd found that secret room. Then we must think about our own team. What if it's someone in the unit?"

They sat in silence for a moment, neither keen to pursue such an unwelcome thought, but understanding they might have to. The spell was broken as Hooley's phone pinged. He glanced at his messages and sat up. It was from his son saying he needed to take a rain check on their dinner tonight. He breathed a heartfelt sigh of relief. He'd totally forgotten he was supposed to be going out.

24

The moment Roper walked into his flat, he felt a compulsion to check the doors and windows for any signs of intrusion. Despite having installed CCTV, he knew he couldn't relax until he'd carried out a physical inspection. He paused to examine the carpet in the hallway — nothing to see. Then a careful study of the open plan living area — also clear. Finally, he looked through the bedrooms and bathrooms. While his flat had three double bedrooms, each with a bathroom, only his own had a bed because he never had anyone to stay and didn't think that would ever change. Of the remaining pair, one was totally bare, while the last had a comfortable chair placed dead centre and thick curtains with black-out blinds. Sometimes he came in here to sit in the darkness and enjoy a sense of total solitude; it helped him calm down after spending time with other people. While the flat was too big for his physical needs, it provided the space he needed to restore his emotional well-being.

"Lovely view you've got here." The voice of the PC surprised him. He noticed that the sun was shining down at such an angle that the light was bouncing back off the river, and the Thames was alive with different types of boats ploughing up and down. The whole thing was framed by the floor-to-ceiling windows. It looked spectacular.

"Oh, yes. Thanks. It is nice. It also looks brilliant at night with all the lights on. It's almost as though the buildings are alive. At least, that's what I think," he added, looking away in case the policemen thought he had said something silly.

Roper moved over to the kitchen area. He only used the kettle, microwave and fridge. He loved eating but had no interest in the process of making food. Opening the refrigerator, he checked the dates on his supply of ready meals. Although they had a day or two on them, they were all thrown away. He had an abiding terror of food poisoning after researching the topic online and being horrified at the potential for becoming severely unwell. He tried to get rid of everything at least two days before the sell-by date.

The PC, who was married with two young children and living in near chaos, marvelled at how immaculate the flat was. Roper thought of his decorative style as minimalist. Others said it was stark. There were no paintings on the wall, no ornaments or mementoes. In the living area was a pair of plain black leather sofas that faced each other, with a smoked-glass coffee table in between. There were no cushions, side tables or lamps. The only other features were the large flat-screen TV, wall-mounted, and a small office table on which he kept his laptop and printer. All his paperwork was stored in the second bedroom. It was the sort of home that looked like someone had just moved in, or maybe moved out.

The uniformed officer enjoyed the view a moment longer then turned to Roper.

"Everything seems fine, so I'll leave you to it. I'll be downstairs when you're ready to go."

Roper heaved a sigh of relief as the man left. He really hated having other people in his private space. It made him feel jittery. This was one space where he could be himself and not feel he was under constant scrutiny. He quickly stripped off his clothing. His shirt and suit were still covered in blood, so he threw them away. He went into the bathroom, turning on the shower before shaving. Then he checked the water temperature; he liked it just short of 'too hot', which meant he had the tap turned to a fraction past the mid-point on the red band. Then he stepped under the pressurised flow and just stood there for ten minutes, enjoying the sensation. Finally, he spent five minutes carefully shampooing and soaping before switching the water to its coldest setting and gasping at the sudden change.

Getting out, he went into his usual energetic drying technique, wincing as he went over his many bruises but determined to stick to his routine. Doing the same things every day was an essential part of the way he prepared to face the world, and his showering ritual was one of the most effective ways to do that. Being in the hospital had deprived him of this necessary process.

He didn't bother checking in the mirror — he knew what he looked like — and padded into the bedroom to pick out a new black suit and white shirt, matched with a black tie. Once dressed, he assembled what he needed for his stay with Hooley. Four more black suits, four more white shirts, four more black ties, plus, of course, an equal number of black socks, polished shoes and white underpants. He would make sure his used outfits were taken straight to the cleaners, ensuring a strict rotation of clothing. Ideally, he would have taken more shoes, but four pairs should be enough, especially as he would be taking his cleaning kit.

With everything packed away in matching black leather travel bags, he carefully made his cup of tea. Six heaped teaspoons of sugar were added to the mug together with three bags of extra-strong tea and then freshly boiled water. This was left to steep for five minutes before the bags were removed and only then adding the milk. The resulting concoction was drunk as rapidly as possible. For some reason, it had the opposite effect it had on most people. Instead of being wired by the combined sugar and caffeine rush, it had a soothing effect.

Then it was time to leave. Picking up his luggage, he left without a backward glance, the front door locking automatically behind him. Reaching the car, he placed his gear in the boot and got into the front passenger seat of the unmarked BMW.

As the policeman began to negotiate the heavy rush-hour traffic, Roper leaned back against the seat. He decided it was time to "reboot". After the attack, he had shut down his emotions. It was the only way he could cope with something so traumatic. Still, now he felt more durable and could allow his feelings back in. However, this was a recent occurrence, and he still needed to tread carefully or risk being overwhelmed. He sometimes thought it wasn't so much that he had no "on" switch; his problem was having no "off" switch.

By the time they arrived in Pimlico he felt he was as close to one hundred per cent as he ever would be, although he doubted if his one hundred per cent was the same as anyone else's. Getting out of the car, he grabbed his stuff and was about to head off when he froze at a sudden thought. He turned back to the car, where the officer was watching him through the open window.

"I forgot to say thank you," he said.

Then he turned and headed off. The man shrugged. He'd been warned that Roper was a bit of an oddball. He stayed where he was until he saw the DCI appear to welcome his guest and only then drove away. He didn't notice the black taxi that had followed them from Tower Bridge and was now parked fifty yards away.

* * *

The "cabbie" watched Roper and Hooley disappear into the building before putting his camera down. He was pretty sure he had got a clear shot of the middle-aged man who had greeted Roper, and now he connected his camera to his phone and emailed the pictures before reporting in with his information. He was congratulated and told to leave the area before anyone noticed him.

25

Dan Sykes was feeling very pleased with himself. It had been his own idea to stake out Roper's property, and now they knew he had moved out. The beating must have shaken him up, as hoped. Studying the set of photographs, he zeroed in on the older man greeting Roper. Presumably, this was Brian Hooley. According to his contact, the DCI was the key to keeping Roper on track. Using his encrypted server, he forwarded the photos to his informant at the Yard with instructions for an urgent identification and more details. If it was Hooley, how could the man afford to live in that part of Pimlico? None of that area was cheap, but it looked like the policeman lived in a prime location.

He swung his feet onto his desk and leaned back in his chair, enjoying the sense of superiority that came from knowing so much about people while they had no idea you existed. He smiled at a sudden thought. Why not send a team in to trash Roper's place over at Tower Bridge? If he was already rattled, that would undoubtedly ramp up the pressure. He decided to use Pat again. He'd done a perfect number on the bean pole and could be entrusted with this next task.

He stood and walked over to a filing cabinet. Opening the top drawer, he pulled out a bottle of Bells and looked at it.

Nothing fancy; it did the job just as well as an expensive single malt. He was a wealthy man and could easily have afforded something from the top of the range, but hated spending money when he didn't have to. He carried the bottle back to the desk and poured a small measure into a glass. He inhaled carefully, and then drank it down quickly. He sat and enjoyed the warming sensation for several minutes. He never drank a lot; he'd seen too many people suffer from excess.

With little else to do, he flicked on the TV. Might as well catch up on the news while he had time on his hands. He took a professional interest in a report on the fighting in Syria. It wasn't that long ago that he'd been out there himself, working as a well-paid mercenary on behalf of the Assad regime. After a few minutes watching the bulletin, he decided there was very little new going on. At least there had been no more news about Sir James, which was a good thing. He was watching the weather report when Pat rang in to receive his instructions. They were short and blunt. "Just smash the door down, make a bit of mess and then scarper. Same drill as before. Make sure he knows about it, but nothing too serious."

He recognised the disappointment in Pat's voice when he told him that Roper wouldn't be there. The man took his work very seriously and once pointed at a target was terrier-like in his determination to see it through.

"I've got a gut feeling this won't be the end of our interest in him. So when it comes time to do him properly, you get the job." Mollified, Pat rang off, saying he would go in after midnight tonight. Sykes decided to go for a run. He still had a few hours to go before he met the latest new arrivals.

* * *

Two hours later he was back in Mayfair. The house wasn't only his office; it was big enough to provide him with accommodation too. He was upstairs, naked, having just come out of the shower, when his contact responded with confirmation that the man in the picture was DCI Hooley.

26

Hooley studied the fistful of spaghetti he was holding in his right hand. Then he looked at Roper and doubled it. He was making his signature dish, the only one he didn't need to refer to a recipe for. Fifty minutes later, a steaming bowl of spaghetti bolognese was placed in the centre of the small dining table. He gave himself a mental pat on the back for cooking extra pasta after watching Roper make short work of two heaped portions, finishing both comfortably ahead of Hooley's single plateful. As he watched his boss finish the final strand of pasta, he said, "I would only eat food that was white when I was younger."

Hooley, who had long ago learned to take Roper's off-beat observations in his stride, was genuinely impressed by this one.

"Really? How did that work, then? It must have been a nightmare for your parents."

"Well, there's milk, I used to drink a lot of that. Potatoes, but only boiled, I didn't like them fried or roasted as they changed colour. Also, some potatoes are quite yellow, so they didn't work. White bread, but no brown crusts, egg whites, most pasta and some white cheese and chicken breast. And there's fish. I used to eat a lot of plain cod." He thought for a moment. "And bananas, so long as they had been peeled first. In fact, bananas and vanilla ice cream, without those black seeds you can get, was my favourite meal."

"But you're OK now. I mean, I've seen you eat all sorts of different-coloured things," he gestured at the remains of the meat sauce in the bowl.

Roper's expression changed, and he stared into the middle distance, something Hooley had learned to recognise as showing he was reviewing the past. Review was the right word to use: Roper's memory had cinematic qualities. He could call up the past and watch it like a TV show. If that wasn't astonishing enough, he had also revealed another factor. His recall mirrored the technology of the moment. This meant his early memories appeared as if on a VHS tape, while the more recent ones were in digital format. Hooley had once speculated that had Roper been born a hundred years earlier his memories would have been on a flickering, black-and-white film reel.

Roper had clearly found what he was looking for. His eyes cleared as he refocussed. "It lasted from when I was five years old to seven years old. I thought anything that was a different colour, like green and red or brown and orange, had a really strong smell. I can't tell you what the smell was like, just that it was an overpowering smell which I hated. White food just smelled like fresh air. My mum, and then my grandmother, tried to make me eat different things, but I refused. Even putting a carrot on my plate used to make me feel sick.

"They used to get really cross and make me sit at the table until I did eat, but I was never going to, and after the first couple of times they gave up. I sat there for two hours once."

Hooley stood up and started to collect the plates and bowl for the dishwasher. "So what happened to get you eating different food?"

Roper smiled. "It was because of Popeye. When I was seven, I started reading the cartoons, and he used to eat spinach to make himself strong. I wanted to be strong, so I did the same. It didn't give me big muscles, though."

Hooley looked at him. "I used to think we had problems getting our kids to eat properly, but compared to you they were little Gordon Ramsays. Still, I can imagine it must have been a day of celebration in your house when you did eat something different." He clapped his hands together. "While I tidy up, why don't you make the tea — I won't have mine as strong as yours — then we can see what's on TV."

* * *

Hooley's phone dragged him out of a deep sleep. He fumbled about and picked it up to see who was calling. It was Roper. Why was he calling if he was in the flat?

"Jonathan, where are you?"

"Outside your door. I didn't know what to do. Someone's broken into my flat."

The DCI sat bolt upright, his heart pounding from being dragged awake. He gave the phone he was holding a puzzled look and then shouted at the door.

"It's OK, Jonathan, come in."

The door opened, and a wild-eyed Roper stood on the threshold. Hooley turned on his bedside light, blinking at the sudden glare. "How do you know your flat is being burgled?"

Roper held his phone up. "My alarm system is linked to my phone, so if there's any problem, it sends me a notification. I've also got CCTV in there so I can see what's happening. There's someone in there now."

Hooley clambered out of bed, glad he was wearing his pyjamas, and looked at the screen on the phone. He could make out a hooded figure that appeared to be throwing objects around. Just then the man looked up at the camera, gave the finger and ran from view. The DCI called 999, giving the operator the details.

He glanced at the time and saw it was just after 3 a.m. He thought about ringing Mayweather but decided it would be best to leave her for a couple of hours. Their priority, for now, was to make sure the intruder had left and then make the flat secure.

"Let me just get some clothes on and I'll drive us over there," he told Roper. He realised the younger man was already dressed, and wondered if he'd been asleep at all.

27

Blue light washed over the entrance to Roper's apartment block. As Hooley pulled up, Roper was already out of his seatbelt and reaching for the door handle. His boss leaned across to gently restrain him by placing a hand on his arm.

"Hold on a minute. If you go charging in there, you're going to alarm the officers inside. We'll go in together, nice and slowly."

Roper looked at him, clearly thinking about shrugging him off. He was breathing hard as if he'd been running. The DCI kept his hand in place a little longer, letting go once he was sure the message had got through. The pair climbed out of the car and Hooley looked around. Even at this hour, there were people about. A couple of young men were standing in the shadows, lured to the possibility of trouble by the police lights. One of them waved a can of lager in mocking salute as they walked up to the entrance of the block.

Roper was glaring in their direction. "Do you think those two might have something to do with the break-in?"

"Not a chance," said Hooley, gripping his arm and pulling him towards the entrance. "Just a couple of pissed-up muppets. Ignore them; we've got better things to do."

At Hooley's insistence, they took the stairs slowly and approached the shattered doorway of Roper's flat. The DCI called out, and a stern-looking policeman appeared and stared at them. The DCI held up his warrant card.

"DCI Hooley. This is my colleague, Jonathan Roper. This is his flat, and we're the ones who called it in."

After checking the ID, the officer visibly relaxed, as did Hooley. He had noted the taser the man was carrying. If Roper had gone charging in, he might well have been shot. The constable turned and called over his shoulder to alert his colleague that all was well. Then he turned back to Roper.

"I take it you've just arrived, sir." He was keeping things formal for now. "How did you know the break-in had happened?"

Roper produced his phone and talked him through the alarm system, pointing out the cameras before showing the brief video clip. The second officer, an older man similar in age to Hooley, was also looking at the clip.

"Friend of yours?" he said as they watched the intruder making a cutting gesture to his throat.

Hooley stepped in before Roper could demonstrate he was an irony-free zone.

"Two days ago, Jonathan was attacked right outside this block. He suffered minor injuries and suspected concussion, so he's staying with me until we're sure he's fully recovered." He gestured at the flat. "Not wishing to state the bleedin' obvious, but I think we have to examine the possibility that the two incidents are related."

The older of the two constables gave him a knowing look.

"Which unit are you attached to, sir?"

"Special Investigations."

"Ah, I see," said the officer. "So, I take it you could tell us what is going on, but then you'd have to kill us afterwards."

Hooley smiled his appreciation at the man's perception. "Something like that. Sorry to keep you in the dark, but my boss would have my guts if I said anything out of turn."

He looked around and then carried on.

"We'll need to arrange for someone to guard this place. Jonathan and I can stay here while I get that in motion, and you guys can get back to some real work."

The older officer nodded. "Fine by us. There's only a couple of patrol units around tonight. It's a good job people don't realise how stretched things can get in the early hours."

The two officers departed, handing over a number for a 24-hour lock-up service that would come and make the flat secure. As soon as they had vanished from view, Roper gave his boss a particularly earnest look.

"That stuff about us killing them. That was a joke? Like the joke about tasering traffic wardens?"

"Well done."

"I don't understand why it's funny, though."

Hooley sighed. Right now, neither could he. "Tell you what, call that emergency number, and then we can go inside to see what damage has been done."

They finally got away just before 6 a.m. The flat had been secured, and Roper had wanted to dash into work, but Hooley insisted they went back to Pimlico to wash and change. He knew it was going to be a long day. He was also quietly impressed at the way Roper was handling it. Although nothing had been taken, the sofas had been slashed and tipped over, and the coffee table was broken. People got upset about a lot less.

28

Mayweather had barely moved during the briefing, but the way her eyes narrowed showed how angry she was.

"You've lived there for almost ten years and never had any problems?"

"Actually, it's been nine years and 252 days," he replied.

Mayweather just stopped herself from saying anything. Roper was nothing if not precise. Tomorrow it would be nine years and 253 days. A lot of people dismissed him because he was pedantic, but he was right, real facts mattered, and she found it engaging that he knew precisely how long he had lived somewhere. She struggled with what day of the week it was.

"Well, I think you've been there long enough to be able to say this sort of thing doesn't happen very often," she concluded. "And I think we're all in agreement that the assault on you and the break-in are related."

Hooley looked at Roper. He wanted to hear what he had to say after he'd had a little while to reflect. "How are you feeling about it? It's one thing sitting around talking about it but quite another to be the victim in all this."

Roper crossed his arms. "I just want to catch the people behind this. They're not going to frighten me." Short, sweet and straight to the point. The two senior officers were relieved.

Mayweather was the first to respond. "One of the many things that concern me is the thought that whoever is behind this could have access to information about how our investigation is going. I mean, Jonathan has barely rejoined the team and he's been targeted twice. But if the plan is to try and upset you, then I think they have seriously underestimated how much you've changed — for the better."

Hooley nodded along. He was about to offer some thoughts of his own when Roper blurted out the word "taxi".

The two stared at him.

"What do you mean, Jonathan?" asked the DCI.

Roper had gone quite still, and Hooley knew he must have been studying a replay of something that happened very recently. Slowly rewinding some part of his memory to check his facts before speaking again. The silence stretched on to become almost uncomfortable before Roper said, "The drive from my flat to Pimlico. There was a taxi behind us all the way." He closed his eyes briefly and nodded before continuing. "I'm fairly certain that we were followed by a London black cab which pulled up when we got to Brian's place."

"A black cab?" said Mayweather. "I don't mean to rain on your parade, but there are thousands of those in London."

Roper nodded. "I've just replayed the journey, and there are things I didn't notice at the time. The driver had a green T-shirt, the light was off, and there was no passenger in the back."

"When you say 'replay', do you mean like replaying a film clip?" she asked.

"Of course," came the somewhat irritable reply. She shook her head. Reading her notes was as close as she ever got to that.

"Are you sure it was the same cab?" she said. "There are all sorts of reasons a driver might not be carrying passengers, and as for green T-shirts, my husband's got one."

Roper closed his eyes again, this time tilting his head back and to the side. The DCI thought that, to all intent, he might have been operating a freeze-frame application.

"No, I'm sure it was the same man. The T-shirt was a V-neck and sort of light green and plain. I couldn't see his face clearly, but he had sloping shoulders, more than most people."

Mayweather wasn't totally convinced, but Hooley was starting to feel more confident.

"A couple of days ago, I saw him locate a hidden room by listening to echoes of me shouting. Being able to remember a taxi is probably a piece of cake."

"OK," she said, deciding to put her doubts to one side. "If you're sure, then I'm going to take it seriously. And that means we need to step up security . . . for both of you. If Jonathan's right, then it means they know where you live as well, Brian. I'm going to organise a security detail on your flat, round the clock, until we know this is over."

They talked about the case a little longer. But once it became apparent there was nothing new to add, Mayweather closed the meeting and said she would come back to them once she had spoken to the chief constable.

"I doubt the patronising bugger can accuse me of over-reacting this time," she said wryly, "but who knows with that man."

* * *

Back at his own desk, Hooley's stomach rumbled. They'd been up most of the night and hadn't eaten. He looked at Roper.

"Don't know about you, but I could eat a scabby horse."

As the words emerged, he realised he had made an error. In a bid to head off the inevitable, he came out with a lame sounding, "Just an expression." It was too late. Roper's eager expression showed he had picked up on the phrase.

"Actually, there are people who eat horse meat; it's very popular in France. I read an article that said many people actually prefer it to beef. They also argue that it gives the animal a proper value at the end of its working life, which ensures they are slaughtered properly. But why would you want to eat a 'scabby' horse? That would be horrible. It might have a disease."

Against his better judgement, Hooley tried to explain. "The idea is that you are so hungry you would eat anything, even a scabby horse."

"Well, that's just stupid." Roper could be quite dismissive when he didn't like what people were saying. Hooley realised he should back away quietly.

"You're right, Jonathan, and I have a much better idea about what to eat. How about a bacon sandwich made from prime pigs? Your choice of ketchup or brown sauce." He was relieved as his diversion tactic worked.

"Brilliant. Are you going to that new organic place?" He beamed as Hooley nodded. "In that case, can I have two of their bacon and sausage sandwiches, with tomato sauce on one and brown sauce on the other?"

For an overweight man, Hooley could be fast on his feet and was out of the door before Roper could say any more.

29

Dan Sykes had a fearsome temper. Over the years he had managed to gain a degree of control over his "anger management issues", but there were times when what he really wanted to do was hurt someone. His rage had driven him to his feet. It took a considerable effort to sit down again. Fighting his temper, he groped around at the back of one of the desk drawers. Finding what he was looking for, he pulled out a sewing needle and without pause rammed it under the nail of the little finger on his left hand. Then he twisted it.

The intense pain felt like it was shooting up into his armpit. He welcomed it. It squashed his temper and brought him back to the moment. Panting, he leaned back in his seat, and the room swam back into view. Then he carefully pulled the pin from under the nail, watching as a thin trickle of blood flowed onto his fingertip.

He stood up again and started pacing round in front of his desk, unconsciously recreating the space he had used for exercise when being held in a Syrian jail. He had spent nine months in solitary after the Assad side, having first employed him, became embarrassed at his brutal tactics. He was held in a room just big enough to hold a rough cot, a bucket and a few spare feet of space. After five minutes, he felt he was back under control. The fury hadn't gone away, and someone was going to suffer later, but for now, he could use it as fuel to sort out his next task. He decided he'd do this job himself.

* * *

The uniformed officer was trying to think of something more boring than guarding an empty house. Even one that had belonged to a murdered billionaire. He decided there wasn't much. Perhaps train spotting — very dull. Watching one of those political broadcasts. And the old favourite, watching paint dry. He bounced gently on his toes; at least he could keep his blood moving. But he'd given up hoping for an urgent shout to call him away. To help pass the time he was keeping a running total of all the delivery vehicles which were coming and going. He'd seen liveried vans from Harrods and Fortnum and Mason, plus a lot of flowers, huge bouquets that probably cost more than he earned in a week. It had taken six people four trips each just to supply flowers to the house four doors down. That was just the stuff he could see. With so many wrapped parcels, he wouldn't have been surprised if someone was delivering drugs or even money and guns.

He watched as a highly polished black Mercedes van parked up, the rear doors facing him. A man dressed in what looked like designer camouflage gear, complete with a peaked cap, jumped out of the passenger side. There was something about the way he moved which drew his attention. It seemed as though the man was operating well within his physical limits, like a boxer just before the start of a fight. He was on his toes and nicely balanced.

The man trotted to the back of the van and opened the doors to get at a large cardboard box. Despite its size, he hefted it easily and moved onto the pavement. The driver appeared, then the two men made their way over to the watching officer.

They stopped in front of him and made a point of looking at the number on the front door and then looking at the delivery sheet. The driver cocked his head, staring at the building. "Got an urgent delivery for a Sir James Taylor," he said. "This is his address, right? We weren't expecting a copper here, though. Been a naughty boy, has he?"

The officer studied the pair. He was incredulous that anybody could be unaware that Sir James Taylor was dead; his brutal murder was still dominating the headlines. Something was also beginning to nibble at his sense of danger. The pair didn't seem like typical delivery men. In fact, now he thought about it, he didn't like the way they were staring at him. There was something predatory about them, and he was starting to feel like the prey.

In an attempt to get on the front foot, he tried to take command. "You need to move on. I'm afraid you're out of luck. This is a crime scene, so there's no way you can deliver that. You're going to have to take that back with you."

The man holding the box looked puzzled. He placed it on the ground and moved closer. His right hand reached into his inside pocket. "I've got more documents here. Came in this afternoon, the order did."

Then he was moving fast, very fast.

* * *

The loaded syringe plunged into the officer's neck. The needle pierced the skin easily. It delivered a lethal dose of a potent nerve agent. As the sharp pain of the injection registered with his conscious brain, his body went into shock. The two men deftly caught him as he started to fall and they pushed into the house, carrying him between them. He was dead by the time they laid him on the floor. Sykes looked down at the body. The eyes were open, but they had the glaze of death. Something he was all too familiar with. A trickle of dirty-yellow foam emerged from the corner of the victim's mouth and ran down his chin.

"Sweet," said Sykes. He rubbed his hands together. He felt much better.

"What are we doing with that?" said the driver, nudging the body with his foot.

"Leave him for his mates to find. That'll get the fuckers hopping about." Sykes set off for the study. "Let's get to it. We should have an hour before his replacement turns up. The boss is mad about us missing the secret room, and he wants us to check it all over again, especially all the books."

30

The call for an "officer down" came as Roper and Hooley were about to set off for Pimlico. They raced round to Eaton Square, arriving to a scene of barely controlled chaos. Armed officers in full protective gear were already in place and in no mood to allow free access. They were finally allowed in, and after suiting-up, Hooley went straight into the house. He didn't notice that Roper was, as usual, taking his time.

The DCI walked inside and saw the body lying, more or less, in the centre of the entranceway. That was where he had been found, and nothing would be touched until the scenes of crime team arrived. Hooley knew only the best people would be working this case. Killing a police officer always triggered a massive response. Hooley was astonished that anyone would risk stirring up such a reaction.

Looking down, he recognised the man as the officer he had shared a joke with just a few days ago. For a moment, his eyes pricked with tears, he was struck by unexpected emotion as he thought of the grief this death would bring to his family and friends. Then he made a deliberate effort to put that to one side; there was work to do if they were going to get the killer.

Roper appeared behind him, stared briefly at the body and then walked into the study. From the hallway, Hooley could see the room had been trashed. All the books had been thrown from the shelves, the furniture, except for the large heavy desk, had been tossed around and even the televisions had been pulled off the walls.

He left Roper staring at the empty bookshelves and joined a uniformed inspector and a grey-faced constable who were in deep discussion. It was clear the PC had discovered the body when he had arrived to replace his colleague. "I only had to take one look to know he was dead."

The man continued, saying he had been surprised not to see his colleague outside on the steps, then noticed the front door was slightly ajar. He assumed he must have been caught short and had gone inside to use the toilet. Pushing inside, he'd seen the body, taken a moment to confirm he was dead and then stepped outside to radio for help. He hadn't been in any other part of the house.

At that point, Roper reappeared and abruptly took over the conversation. Wasting no time on introducing himself, he simply launched into an explanation. "I've concluded that the officer was attacked outside by at least two men. He was given a lethal injection and then dragged in here as he was dying. The men dumped his body here in the hallway and then went to search Sir James's study but found nothing."

In the silence that followed Hooley tried to think of what to say but was beaten to it by the inspector, who glared at Roper. "Can I remind you that this is a crime scene? We don't need some clown jumping in with whatever theory is flitting around inside his head. How could you possibly have worked all that out? You've only been here a few minutes."

Roper looked puzzled, and Hooley took the opportunity to try to calm things down. "Actually, Jonathan, I really need you to go through that again, and this time don't leave anything out. I want us all to hear what you've seen that has led to your conclusions." He held up a hand as Roper went to reply. "Right from the very start please."

Roper nodded several times and then started to explain.

"Two days ago, Chief Inspector Hooley and I met the officer when we came to inspect the house. I realised then he was quite a big man as he was my height but much more heavily built.

"For someone to have overcome him easily, it would have to involve a weapon, like a gun or knife, but the information coming over the radio as we made our way here said that wasn't the case. That led me to set up a working theory that he may have been drugged.

"When we arrived, I immediately saw there were black scuff marks on the ground outside the door. There are two lines of marks, suggesting he had been dragged backwards with his heels scraping on the ground. For such a big man, it would have taken at least two people to drag him."

Roper stopped and looked at his audience. *Good man,* thought the DCI, *you're giving people a chance to take the information on board. At least some of the lessons are working.*

Roper walked over and knelt by the side of the body. He pointed to the right of the victim's throat. "As soon as I walked in, I saw that he had been injected in the neck. In fact, it was directly into the carotid artery, so whatever was in there would have started to work almost instantaneously as it was pumped straight round his body. My guess is that it was a nerve blocker of some sort. Another thing I noted was the traces of foam on his lips, which supported my theory."

Hooley watched the inspector looking down at the body. Now it had been pointed out, the injection mark was clear, but the foam was very faint. The officer looked up, his expression turning to grudging acceptance.

Hooley smiled his approval. "You also mentioned that they were looking for something but didn't find it."

"That's right," Roper said. "They were rechecking the bookcase again, but all the books are there, even if they have been thrown about the room."

The DCI was taken aback. "There's a small library in there. Even by your standards, that's an impressive recall."

Roper was starting to explain when the inspector cut across him. "Are you Jonathan Roper?"

Roper just shrugged, unsure why he was being asked. Hooley stepped in. "As Jonathan has just demonstrated, he has some remarkable investigative skills. I'm sure we'll get confirmation that he's right. I'd also like to remind you that this is a case for the Special Investigations Unit."

This seemed to tip the inspector over the edge, and he launched into a protest about it being one of his men who was the victim. Hooley was sympathetic. In the circumstances, he would have reacted the same way. Still, he needed to get this under control before it turned into a pissing contest. If there was one thing his boss hated it was rivalries between different police teams. "I understand. He's one of yours, and that hurts. But believe me, I will do this the right way. We owe it to his family to make sure we do everything we can."

At the mention of family, the inspector's shoulders slumped, and the fight seemed to go out of him. "He and his wife had a little girl a couple of months ago. She brought the baby into the station a few weeks back. He was so proud of her."

Hooley stayed silent. There was nothing he could say or do that would make the job of breaking the news any easier. His phone pinged, and he saw it was a message from Mayweather to say she was minutes away.

"Roper and I need to get on with checking through the house. We were here a couple of days ago, so that should help. Our boss is on her way as well."

The man appeared to overcome his initial shock over the loss of his colleague. "Of course."

After another look at the study, they made a tour of the house but found nothing else. As they walked back down the stairs, Hooley was pleased to see both Julie Mayweather and the pathologist had arrived. The medic immediately pointed to the site on the dead policeman's neck. He supported Roper's opinion as to the cause of death.

"Can you give us any thoughts on time of death?" Mayweather asked.

The doctor didn't immediately reply. Instead, he carefully checked around the face and neck of the murdered officer then sat back on his haunches and levered himself up. It looked like a painful process, and beads of sweat broke out on his forehead. He carefully removed his protective gloves, revealing surprisingly dainty hands, all the while seemingly oblivious to Mayweather's barely suppressed irritation. When he finally spoke, he had a faint Welsh accent.

"Your boy here — his body temperature hasn't dropped much, so I'd be inclined to say he was killed less than two hours ago."

Hooley grimaced. The fact that his killer, or killers, may have been recently standing right where he was, added to his sense of anger.

As they left Roper asked Hooley why the inspector had name-checked him.

"Let's just say you're getting quite a reputation in the Met."

31

Eaton Square was teeming with police. Even some off-duty officers had reported in. They were part of a substantial door-to-door effort, canvassing witnesses and collecting footage from the multiple CCTV systems in the area. With Sir James's house serving as the epicentre, the activity rippled out like an expanding shock wave. Soon teams were working their way out beyond the square itself. Roper was assigned to taking an overview of the information pouring in and told to chase up any aspect that struck him as potentially useful.

To his frustration, none of the CCTV showed any clear shots of the attackers. Camera angles and the caps the killers were wearing combined to hide their faces. Roper showed Hooley a clip taken from a camera next door to Sir James's house, running it on a laptop he'd scrounged up from somewhere.

"You can see how they make sure never to look directly at the camera," he said, pointing at the images. "This footage also confirms what I thought. There were two men, and they acted very fast. Even if someone had seen it happen, they might not have registered what was going on."

This was true — despite looking several times, Hooley could only just make out what happened. "Have we got anything on their vehicle?" he asked.

Roper called up another piece of film and tapped the screen as a van came into view. "Again, there's no shortage of film, but the windows are tinted, and even the windscreen is pretty dark. There is some software that might help sharpen the images, but I don't think it will help us very much. We've got a number plate, but I doubt it will lead anywhere."

Mayweather shook her head. "What sort of people are we dealing with? It's almost as though killing a policeman in broad daylight is nothing to them."

Roper had been waiting for the right moment to show them the next bit. "I think this sums up what we are up against." He reset his laptop and inched the images forward while talking them through what they were looking at. "As you can see, the two men walk up. They're turned slightly from the camera and stay that way. There's some sort of conversation, and then the closest man puts his box on the ground. Now, I'll just hold it there for a moment and then count down what happens next."

He hit the play button. "One." As he spoke the man straightened up, reached into his jacket and produced a hypodermic.

"Two." The needle was plunged into the officer's neck, and the plunger depressed.

"Three." The two men were either side of the policeman, dragging him inside the house.

Roper stopped the film.

"In just three seconds, it's all over. They've administered the drug and got our man out of sight. There's no hesitation at all, and the needle is perfectly placed into the carotid artery. Plus, notice how calm everything is. They've clearly done this sort of thing before, most likely military training or even special forces."

Hooley spoke up. "Perhaps we need to be talking to our own military?"

"Good idea," said Mayweather. "Jonathan's right to flag this up. If we've got mercenaries running around in London, then we're going to need all the support we can get."

"Brian, can you start with the anti-terror squad and then talk to Special Branch and MI5? In fact, make sure we get some sort of liaison with the SAS as well. It may well be that one of those can help us identify who these characters are."

She turned her attention back to Roper. "Sharp analysis there, Jonathan. I'm sure we'd have got there eventually, but you keep getting to the heart of things, and you're doing it quickly. Is there anything else you want to discuss?"

He shook his head.

"In that case, get wrapped up here as soon as you can. It's almost 8 p.m., and taking a break for food and sleep is a good idea."

Roper wasn't good at reading people, but knew enough to understand when Mayweather was telling him what to do.

32

The tantalising smell of spices wafted through the evening air as they approached the Balti House. The familiar, mouth-watering aroma was almost enough to drive away the memories of Eaton Square. The restaurant was a short walk from Hooley's flat and was the perfect spot when he didn't feel like cooking. It was late, and customers were already leaving as they arrived, so they had no trouble getting a table.

In the last couple of years, the restaurant had undergone a makeover, and there was no trace of the original flock wallpaper that had served since the early 1980s. While there was no doubt the new look was contemporary and comfortable, Hooley had been known to profess nostalgia for the previous decoration, especially after a couple of beers.

The DCI managed to get his drink order in before they had sat down, so a pint of lager arrived almost as soon as he made himself comfortable. Roper was sticking to water. He glanced at the menu but he'd already made his choice: a lamb rogan josh with a bowl of double-sized pilau rice, sag bhaji, an onion bhaji and a Peshwari naan as his sides. It was the meal he always ate. As far as he was concerned, if you liked a particular food, then stick with it.

Hooley watched him put the menu down. "I envy you sometimes. The trouble for me is that I like everything they do here."

Roper drained his glass of water. "You should go for a tandoori kebab. You don't really want something with a sauce because, apart from it being calorific, at your age you need to watch out for rich, spicy food. You'll be up half the night with indigestion. Plus, all the fat will have a negative impact on your cholesterol and combined with the sugars will make you more susceptible to diabetes, cancer, heart disease or stroke. Also, combining fats and sugars late at night will impact your sleep, which will make it harder for you to do your job properly tomorrow because you will be too run down."

Statement over, he took another sip of water and looked at Hooley. The DCI had frozen with his pint inches from his mouth. For some reason, he had lost his appetite. He managed to force the glass to his lips and took a long, calming swallow. As he put the glass down, he sighed. Roper might sound like a terrifying health commercial, but he was right. By the time the food arrived, it would be almost 10 p.m., far later than he usually ate.

"Much as I hate to say it, you may have a point."

Roper looked as though he had more to add, so the DCI held up his left hand. "Just because you are right about something, it doesn't give you carte blanche to turn it into a lecture. The way you told me would upset most people. I know you as well as anyone, and I was taken aback."

A combination of tiredness and irritation made him speak more sharply than he intended. Roper looked worried, and Hooley realised he needed to tread more carefully. A lot of people complained that Roper suffered from a thick-skinned insensitivity, but the DCI knew this wasn't true. Hooley tried to think of a way to turn the argument into a positive.

"I tell you what, let me explain this tomorrow. It's been a long day, and we both need to relax a little, but I will take time with you over a cup of tea. And just to prove I do listen to your advice, I'll have a small chicken kebab with salad and yoghurt sauce on the side."

He called the waiter over to place their order and decided another lager would be good as well. He was being good, but not that good. As they waited, Hooley kept the conversation on football. An easy task given Roper was an obsessive Chelsea fan who had an endless supply of statistics about his team including, to Hooley's dismay, a huge collection charting the current advantage that Chelsea held over his team, Arsenal. After the food arrived, they ate in silence. Once everything was cleared, Hooley looked at his colleague. There was one thing he wanted to raise before they headed home.

"You seemed to cope well with seeing the body at Eaton Square. Are you still feeling OK or do you need to talk about it?"

Roper looked thoughtful. "I'm fine. Those weeks I spent at the hospital morgue really helped. They taught me to realise that a body needed to be treated respectfully and that we need to do our best for the victim and their family."

Hooley nodded. "Well done, that's exactly the right attitude. But, I tell you what, I've seen so many bodies over the years I've decided I want to be cremated. I really don't fancy being put in the ground and left to rot."

"That's just being superstitious," said Roper, as blunt as always. "I've already arranged for a woodland burial so my body can help to provide nutrition for a tree. That's the most effective way of using it."

The DCI held his hands out in a conciliatory gesture. "I guess we'll just have to agree to disagree on that one."

33

Hooley jabbed the keyboard so hard he accidentally hurt himself. The lack of recent progress was making him restless. It didn't help that he had spotted the irony; here he was, the big tough detective, losing the plot while his supposedly vulnerable colleague was serenely working away.

There had been a brief flurry of excitement first thing this morning when it was reported that the van used at Eaton Square had been found. It had been abandoned on one of the narrow streets at the back of the Peter Jones department store on Sloane Square. But the mood had quickly evaporated as the crime techs reported that someone had done a forensically expert job of removing any evidence. The vehicle had been methodically wiped down with bleach. They would keep at it but weren't holding out a great deal of hope.

Meanwhile, the team had trawled hours of CCTV footage but were still unable to get a clear image of the two men. The much-hyped new software hadn't been able to help. It had lightened the images, but they were still blurry. Even Roper, who could generally be relied on to stick with a task to the bitter end, had decided to move on. He said he would be better off pursuing the biotech side of the investigation, as he still hadn't managed to get stuck into the details they had found in the secret room.

As the investigative pace slowed, Hooley had to fight the urge to interfere in what everyone was doing and start micro-managing. He knew if he did that he would only slow things down. Both he and Julie Mayweather had carefully selected the unit members based on their outstanding skills. The last thing they needed was to feel the boss was perched on their shoulder. On an investigation like this, he knew no one would be giving less than their best. So that left his keyboard in prime position for some punishment. Consequently, he had been thumping away until he had realised his stubby fingers were hurting.

Feeling embarrassed, he sneaked a look at Roper to see if he had noticed and saw he was — as usual — too engrossed to take any interest. When his mobile went off a moment later, he felt a sense of relief — his keyboard at least could catch a break. It was his anti-terror squad contact, Bill Nugent.

"Sounds like the SAS boys" — he pronounced it "sass" — "have got something for you. I've just spoken to a Major Tom Phillips. I'll text you his number so you can call him directly. He says he wants to come in and see you. He's in London so it's not as if you'll have to wait for him to come down from Hereford or wherever."

An hour later the major arrived. Hooley had only had limited dealings with Special Forces so was intrigued to find out what the man was like. The major was about his height, maybe a little taller, and dressed casually in jeans, a plain T-shirt and trainers. Judging his age was impossible. Anything from mid-twenties to forty. He was clearly in top shape — very lean, with crystal-clear blue eyes, a shaved head and a firm handshake, which the DCI suspected could be a lot firmer if the man wanted to make a point.

Roper seemed especially fascinated to meet the major and had leapt up to shake hands, something quite unusual as he usually shied away from physical contact. The major took the seat in front of Hooley's desk and declined an offer of coffee with a rueful grin.

"I love coffee, but I try to limit it to two cups a day. I'm already on my fifth so, with regret, I'll have to turn your offer down."

Hooley found himself warming to the man. When he glanced at Roper, he was amused to see he was gazing admiringly at the major.

The SAS officer suddenly looked serious. "Best get down to business. We've identified one of the people in the photos, and we think we may have a line on the other one as well."

He took a breath as Hooley looked on expectantly. "The man who killed the policeman is called Dan Sykes, and he is one of ours — or, I should say, used to be one of ours. He disappeared back in 2006. He was about to be arrested for major-league crimes. He was selling millions of pounds' worth of looted artefacts from Iraq. After he vanished, we discovered he had been building a mini empire that dealt in everything from human trafficking to gun-running, drugs and extortion. And that's just the shortlist.

"We've been trying to track him down ever since, but he always manages to stay one step ahead. He was in Syria for a while, earning big bucks, but that went sour. He ended up in prison and it was looking grim until he managed to grease a few palms and quietly disappear. Despite that set back he's still a wealthy man. Since Syria he's been super careful, buying himself an intelligence network to ensure he knows what he's getting into. I know the images you sent us aren't the greatest, but I would recognise that bastard anywhere. The only surprise is that he's resurfaced in London. We were under the impression he was somewhere in South America.

"One of my men also thinks he recognised the other one; they only met briefly, but he thinks he's French. His first name is Pat, but he's also known as 'French Pat' for obvious reasons. I've taken the liberty of sending the footage to our contacts in the French military. Hopefully, we will learn something soon."

He stopped talking and reached into his pocket to pull out a flash drive.

"This is what we have on Sykes, including pictures. But as you'll see, they were taken 10 years ago. I recognised him as much from the way he moves as anything else. He was almost obsessive about how he controlled his body, so he didn't waste energy. Some Special Forces guys can be like that, but Sykes really stood out."

34

Julie Mayweather's expression darkened as her deputy outlined the briefing they had received from the SAS major.

"We asked him about the attack on Roper, and he was very concerned," said the DCI. "He said that type of beating is notoriously difficult to do without really hurting people. You either need to be very lucky or very good at what you are doing."

He could see she was mulling over what she'd been told. After a few moments, she asked the question which was on everybody's mind.

"So, if we accept that the attack on Jonathan was a warning, why suddenly escalate to killing a police officer?"

Hooley leaned forward in his chair. "The major said we needed to look at it in more than one way. First, the killing of one of our own automatically becomes a priority issue, which swallows up investigative resources. Our enemy would know perfectly well that we'll throw everything at solving the murder.

"He also said the escalation in violence means they may well have adjusted the time frame they're operating to. When they attacked Roper, they probably thought time was on their side, but now, for whatever reason, they need to speed things up."

Mayweather rubbed her temples. "This paints an alarming picture of who we're dealing with and the methods they might use to cover their tracks." She held a tight expression on her face. "Was there anything else from Major Phillips?"

Now it was the DCI's turn to look concerned. "He feels that some of us may be in danger."

"I take it you mean yourself and Jonathan?"

Hooley saw her glance at Roper to see how he felt about this, but couldn't read the expression on his face.

"You as well," he continued. "It's all about 'chopping off the head', apparently. The major's convinced the attack on Jonathan proves our men have good intelligence on us, so we must prepare for the worst. He's offered to provide protection."

This appeared to hit home with Mayweather. She looked directly at Hooley. "What do you think? Are we really in that much danger?"

"I hate to say it, but I think we may be."

She turned to Roper. "Jonathan, what's your view?"

"I think the major made perfect sense," he said to the evident surprise of Mayweather. "If they're suddenly speeding up the time frame, then they would want to disrupt our leadership team. Attacking you and Brian would create confusion and slow down our investigation. My view is that we accept the major's offer of help. If the other side is Special Forces trained, we need to match that. And it will make them think hard about attacking us again."

Hooley was nodding along. Mayweather asked, "What about your wife, Brian? I think we have to assume that she may well be at risk until this is brought under control."

He leaned back in his seat and grimaced. "I know, I'd been thinking about that. We haven't spoken for six months, at least not without shouting, so I fear she'll go mad when I ring her up to say there's a protection team on the way."

Mayweather nodded sympathetically. "Do you think it might help if I ring to break the news? It keeps the blame off you, and then you can speak once she's had a chance to absorb everything."

Hooley felt a wave of relief and nodded his thanks at her suggestion.

She turned back to Roper. "So, what do you want to do while all this is being set up?"

"I think it's time I tried out my new rainbow spectrum."

35

Mayweather couldn't resist a quick glance at her deputy and was pleased to note that he clearly had no idea what Roper was talking about either, so at least she wasn't going to be the odd one out. Even as this thought settled, Roper said, "Richard of York gave battle in vain." He beamed at her, then added, "Red, orange, yellow, green, blue, indigo and violet — those are the main colours of the rainbow, and that's the mnemonic to remember them by. Well actually there's a bit of an argument about that, and that's why it's taken me a couple of days to get through it."

He was warming to his theme, his eyes sparkling. He was also blinking rapidly, a sure sign that he was thinking fast and furiously as he ran through the details. His audience had no idea what he was talking about but were hoping that, if they allowed him to plough ahead, it would start to make sense.

Roper continued. "The light we can see is on a spectrum," he said, drawing an imaginary horizontal line in the air. "There are said to be a hundred different colours, maybe more, although most people can't make out anything like that many. And that's not counting things like infra-red, which nobody can see.

"Then there's the linguistic argument: does everyone actually see the same colours? So, is the blue I see the same as your blue? Or do we describe colours in the same sort of way since they may mean different things to different people? Some people can even see sounds as colours."

He leaned forward to emphasise his point, his hands seemingly taking on a life of their own as they traced patterns in the air. "To make the discussion more manageable, people generally talk about the 'primary colours of the rainbow'. There are seven overall, although there is quite an argument about whether indigo is really a primary. Of course, you get other factors that come into play. Even the primary colours can be variable if you get something like 'spectral smearing' . . ."

As he drew breath to carry on, Hooley jumped in. "Jonathan." He spoke quite loudly. Roper stopped talking and looked startled. The DCI pressed his advantage. "I think we might find it easier to understand if you tell us what you have in mind first, then you can go into the theory later — much later, preferably."

Roper frowned. "Yes, I suppose I could do that, but it really is fascinating when you get into it. There are all the myths about rainbows, like the idea that you can find a pot of gold . . ."

"Jonathan . . ." Hooley gave him a very direct look.

Roper ran his hand through his hair and let out a deep sigh. "The point is that my new rainbow spectrum will allow me to process information better. You see, I started thinking that if I placed information in different coloured boxes, I could then put the same information in more than one box if I thought there might be links."

Mayweather slowly placed her hand in the air, as if trying to attract the teacher's attention in school. She was torn between hearing more theory and needing more practical information.

"Yes?" Roper looked impatient.

"I take it these coloured boxes are in your head — they're imaginary. Or have you got a set of boxes somewhere?"

"Of course they're imaginary," said Roper. "Why would I want real boxes?"

"I just wanted to be sure. Anyway, go on. I interrupted you."

Roper shook his head, obviously collecting his thoughts.

"It's quite hard to explain, really. To be honest, I don't fully understand it, I just know that it works. That's why I've taken so long to tell you about it." He was looking at his shoes, a habit he had got into when trying to explain how his mind worked. It meant he could avoid making eye contact.

"This is something I've been thinking about since my suspension. While I was at home and had a lot of time to think I began to realise that I could assign a colour to a piece of information, or even more than one colour. Then as I get more colour-coded information, I can see which of the colours are close together on the spectrum. Blue and indigo can hold the same piece of information, for example, but at the same time link to other bits of information in that colour box. It means the same item can have more than one meaning or connection to something else."

He carried on, oblivious that Mayweather was now wearing the desperate smile of someone who had accidentally wandered into a lecture about quantum mechanics when they'd been expecting a slide show about common garden plants.

Roper said, "At first, I was using the full spectrum of colour variations, or at least the ones we know about. But that became too confusing because I had so many boxes, I couldn't hold all the links in my mind. That's when I started thinking about rainbows. You see, if you whittle it down to primary colours, then it starts to make sense." He looked up expectantly.

Hooley looked at his Mayweather and raised his eyebrows. She fought back a desire to laugh. She was determined to see this through. "In your mind, you've created seven different-coloured boxes, the primary colours of the rainbow."

Roper nodded back.

"And you can store information in one or more of those boxes. And that helps how?"

"Well, if my theory is right, it will let me see how everything fits together. I believe this will unveil the patterns to show me what is really happening or about to happen."

She noted Hooley was rubbing his temple. She sincerely hoped there was going to be gold at the end of this rainbow. "So, what are your boxes telling you now?"

The look she received showed that Roper thought she hadn't been keeping up. "Nothing, of course. How could they be? As I thought I just explained to you, I am only now at the stage where I can bring it into play."

Roper left to get coffee and Hooley turned to his boss.

"I suppose there's one benefit of having your own SAS man on standby. If all else fails, I can ask him to shoot me."

36

Hooley couldn't shake off a sense of mounting danger. He had never known anything like it. Over the years he had been on the receiving end of many a threat, but most were delivered in the heat of the moment and then disappeared as tempers cooled. This was different, as though someone had changed the rules of the game.

The DCI felt he was being dragged out of a world he understood and into something entirely different and unsettling. It wasn't helping that Roper had come up with his rainbow spectrum. If he was being honest, he hadn't understood what he was talking about. Information with multiple meanings sounded a bit esoteric to him. He was glad he wasn't going to have to explain it to anyone else.

But then if he'd wanted an easy life, he would never have backed Roper in the first place. He'd gone out on a limb to get him back and was still convinced it would be worth it. He also took considerable comfort from the fact that Roper was making such an effort to explain himself. It was a process that seemed to have followed his suspension. Hooley didn't underestimate how difficult this must have been for him. Over the years, he'd learned how Roper had been ridiculed at school, and later at work when he had tried to explain the way his mind worked. With the benefit of hindsight, the DCI could now see that the paedophilia investigation was probably the point at which Roper had started to improve the way he communicated. He had come up with a surprisingly detailed analysis which had allowed them to pinpoint who the key people were. Until his intervention, they had been looking in all the wrong places, so that the focus was on the minor players — men who needed locking up, but not the puppet master himself.

But this flash of insight had been swiftly followed by a crisis that came close to bringing everything crashing down. He had to trust Roper was now in a stronger place emotionally. Hooley was honest enough to realise that part of the reason he looked out for Roper was that he couldn't help thinking of him as a surrogate son. It allowed him a degree of payback for the guilt he felt over not being around enough for his own children. They'd turned out fine, but he had regrets, especially over the key events he'd missed.

He puffed out his cheeks. He couldn't afford to spend too much time on introspection. While he did need to keep a careful watch on Roper, he also had a complex investigation to run and couldn't take his eye off the ball.

His phone rang, loudly intruding on his thoughts. The pathologist Kirsty Goodchild was on the line.

"Just to let you know, we've confirmed that the dog blood found was some sort of mastiff, which could be anything from a lovely little Staffordshire bull terrier to a great big pit bull. But at least your film and my blood match up." She rang off after telling him it was high time he bought her a drink. "If you want to settle up, just send me a crate of a nice unoaked Chardonnay for Christmas." He could imagine her grinning as she put the phone down.

37

"If they're using a sniper there may not be much we can do for you, apart from hose everything down afterwards."

The Special Forces soldiers seemed to have their own brand of humour. The comment was delivered with an incongruously cheerful smile by Spike, the second of the two SAS minders who had been sent to keep a watch on Roper and Hooley. To Hooley's eye, Spike and his colleague Dave were close to identical. Tough-looking men with short-cropped hair and a calm demeanour, very similar to their superior, Major Phillips. Spike was the more talkative of the two and had been explaining the practical limits of what they could do.

"I can do this," he said, demonstrating an ability to raise his leg straight up so that his foot went over his head, then adding. "But I can't see around corners. So, if the bad guys are lurking, we need to be really, really careful." Throughout this, he had kept his balance on one foot, but now he brought his raised leg back down.

He went on. "We're taking the view that while you're at work, you're going to be as safe as you can be. No security is ever foolproof, not even for American presidents. The US Secret Service boys are still having the piss taken after they allowed Ronald Reagan to be shot. They get a bit touchy about it, but whatever they say, it was a balls-up. That's something we like to remind them about as often as possible.

"But I digress. The point is that while you two are at work, you are surrounded by people, many of whom may have weapons or at least access to weapons. So, if it was me, I would rule out attacking you at your office."

Spike's manner was jaunty without being cocky, something that the DCI assumed was down to a combination of attitude and training. The SAS man winked at Roper as he went on.

"We're going to concentrate on keeping an eye out while you're at your home or at the restaurants you might visit. Sometimes people hate having security around, and it's not our normal bag, but we know the ropes, and the boss says that since it's one of ours that's causing you problems, fair enough. Hopefully, no one's going to be roughing you up in the street again if we're around. Our ugly mugs are usually enough to keep anyone at bay."

He looked at Hooley and grinned.

"The boys assigned to your wife have been in touch. She's already given them quite a bollocking, so they know they've got to mind their language. They say that if anyone gets past them, they're going to end up regretting it. Your missus will make mincemeat of them."

Hooley nodded with conviction. From personal experience, he knew that his wife could put a frying pan to uses that were not advertised by the manufacturer. At the same time, he felt a shred of guilt. It was his job that was putting her at risk. She'd take it in her stride, he was sure, but in the long run, it was going to be another thing that divided them.

As the SAS men left, Roper asked them if there was any advice they would give to make sure they got through the next few weeks safely.

"There is one thing," said Spike. "If one of us says 'get down' it would be very helpful if you did it straight away. You'd be amazed at how many people seem to think that 'get down' means standing there looking puzzled. If we shout 'get down' it's because we think somebody might be about to start shooting at you."

After they left, Hooley looked at Roper for a moment. "Are you OK with all this, Jonathan? They're obviously taking this seriously, so we're going to have to be careful."

Roper seemed quite energised. "I think this is the right decision. If we must have guards, then statistically we're going to be much safer with the SAS than anyone else. I also think the best thing we can do is to concentrate on solving this case, so we no longer need protection."

Hooley thought there was no arguing with that, and his mind turned to more down-to-earth matters. All this talk of mincemeat and frying pans had made him feel hungry. "We need to sort out a restaurant for tonight. That Italian I mentioned is just a short walk from the flat. If I let Spike know, he can decide if it's safe for us to go, or whether he'd rather we got a delivery at the flat. If he says yes, it's perfect for a glass of red and a bowl of pasta."

"What if I don't want pasta?" asked Roper, with a slight frown.

"Don't worry, they do have other choices. I was just trying to make a point that it is a lovely place and very relaxed. I am quite sure you will like it . . ."

Hooley tailed off. He was now talking to the top of Roper's head, the younger man having lost all interest once he'd heard there were other choices and returned to studying his computer screen. Spike was happy with their plan, offering one note of caution. The DCI rang the restaurant to make the booking for 8 p.m. He was about to ring off when he remembered Spike's advice. "Not near the window, please."

38

Dan Sykes carefully placed his phone on the desk. There were times, like now, when he wished he could do without it. How much simpler would life be if he could just get on without being disturbed? But he had lost the right to make his own decisions when he had sold out to Tommy Burton, and that was why he was sitting in Mayfair waiting for his boss to decide whether to show up. He'd said five minutes half an hour ago.

Sykes stopped staring at his mobile and instead switched his attention to the CCTV cameras that monitored the front of the property. He settled back in the chair as he watched the street scene outside. At precisely 11 a.m. a black Range Rover pulled up directly opposite the front door, blocking access for any other vehicle. The front passenger door opened and a man jumped out, scanning the surrounding area before opening the rear passenger door. Burton was a big unit, just over six feet three inches tall and heavily built with the shoulders of a professional boxer. From previous meetings, Sykes had guessed his weight to be slightly north of 200 pounds, with no trace of fat. He had piercing blue eyes, and his thick brown hair was trimmed short. He was also a sharp dresser. That made-to-measure suit must have set him back four figures.

He strode to the front door, glancing up at the camera as he approached. Although it was the briefest look, it was ample time for the extraordinary charisma he possessed to be projected through the lens. Sykes was not a man easily impressed, but there was no doubt about it; his boss had an aura about him. With a brilliant smile that showed off an impressive set of teeth, it was hard to reconcile the welcoming image with the reality. As Sykes was acutely aware, this man was one of the most cold-blooded people he had encountered, as capable of ordering a killing as he was requesting a cup of tea.

A few seconds later Burton pushed open the door to the office. He paused on the threshold and carefully looked around, as if he was checking for a trap. Then, apparently satisfied, he stepped into the room. Sykes was already standing, careful to signal his respect. He had learned long ago that allowing any sign of rebellion to show was a mistake, especially with men as finely tuned to insult as Burton. It was odd how many alpha-male types could be so thin-skinned.

He waited patiently, his arms crossed in front of him. He was usually able to read people's body language, but he could never do that with this man. Burton appeared totally self-contained and never gave away the slightest hint of his true feelings. Sykes had read somewhere about psychopaths having a remarkable ability to mask their emotions. They could be at the point of murdering someone, and the victim would never suspect anything was wrong. It helped explain Burton.

Sykes himself was making such an effort to maintain a neutral expression it was making his face ache. But he was determined not to let discomfort show. The silence between the two men continued to grow. It was starting to feel like one of those TV shows where the presenter overdoes the big build-up before announcing who's departing this week. Finally, the man made a small movement, tilting his head ever so slightly to the left.

"They know who you are."

It wasn't what he'd been expecting to hear. Not because he didn't expect to get recognised but because he hadn't expected to hear it from this man. He was momentarily confused, then his brain worked out what had just been said. Sykes ground his teeth. Damn the man and his stupid mind games.

"I take it you mean the police," he managed to speak calmly. He gathered his thoughts. "They were always going to figure it out eventually. I suppose the only surprise is how fast they've been."

"It was Roper who worked out you must have been ex-military. It seems your *little attempt* to knock him off his stride failed to have the desired effect."

The way he emphasised "little attempt" left Sykes in no doubt that he was being reprimanded. It also reminded him that Burton had access to good information about the police. He wondered how senior his contact — or contacts — were.

"The problem now is that they have protection in place, so you can't try that again." Burton jabbed a finger at him to underline the point. Sykes kept silent. As far as he was concerned, the effectiveness of any protection was determined by the ability of the people doing it. But if he got into that conversation, he'd be inviting further criticism. While he was thinking, his boss had clasped his hands behind his back and turned to walk over to the window before executing a neat about-turn and pacing back to stand in front of the desk again. Sykes just managed to keep a sneer off his face. Did the prick think he would be the slightest bit impressed by this grandstanding? It was a long time since he'd been on a parade ground.

Burton stared at him. "I want to move the schedule up again. You now have two weeks to get everything done."

Sykes had been told he had four weeks just the previous day. Something must be going wrong to suddenly speed things up. He'd love to know what but knew better than to ask. He wouldn't give the man the opportunity to tell him he was too junior to need to know the answer.

"We can handle that," he said, with considerably more confidence than he genuinely felt. There was a lot to do, and two weeks would leave no room for delays or mistakes. Then he realised his boss was making no attempt to leave. There must be something else. He waited patiently.

"One of the researchers needs picking up. I'll explain why later, but she must be treated carefully. Under no circumstances is she to be harmed — at least, not yet."

Before he turned to leave his boss reached into the inside pocket of his jacket and pulled out a photograph, which he tossed onto the desk.

"This is her. I'd like it done in the next two days."

After his boss left, Sykes picked up the photograph. He saw a young woman, not pretty but with a friendly smile. He wasn't given to sentimentality, but she reminded him a little of his sister's daughter. While his niece was a few years younger, she shared the same self-confident appearance. Sykes shrugged as he flipped the picture over. The woman's address was on the back, so that saved him having to dig one out. It made no difference to him what happened to her. He just needed to think about how he was going to play this one.

39

The house boasted a bay window and a tiny front garden just big enough to accommodate a pair of terracotta pots filled with a mix of pale-pink geraniums and blue lavender. The three-bedroom property was part of a mid-Victorian terrace in the triangle of streets created by drawing a line connecting the tube stations at Barons Court, West Brompton and Parsons Green. Years ago, this would have been described as yuppie central, and it still spoke of money. Most of the properties in this street had remained family homes rather than suffering the indignity of being chopped into flats. Many, including this one, had been extended into the roof, creating a third floor.

French Pat was sitting in a blue Ford Mondeo parked a few doors away. It gave him a clear view of the front door. Dan Sykes had given him all the details, and just after 6 p.m. his target, Tricia Jenkins, had arrived home and let herself in. Although it was mid-summer, dense, dark clouds overhead made it gloomy for the time of year, and he could mark her progress from the lights she turned on as she headed upstairs. He noted she spent several minutes on the third floor before the light went off, and moments later she stepped out of the front door dressed in running gear.

Unaware of her watcher, she went into a vigorous stretching routine that was much admired. He thought she looked fit and lithe, and he liked the way she kept her hair cut short. It looked boyish and suited her high cheekbones. The stretches over, she headed out of the gate and turned right in the general direction of Fulham Broadway. Setting a good pace, she rapidly disappeared from view.

Pat decided this was his moment. He walked up to the door, careful to look like he belonged. It really was amazing what people failed to notice if you were confident about your actions. His set of picks made short work of the lock, and he was inside. He waited for the tell-tale beeping of the alarm counting down, but there was silence. This did not surprise him. Experience had taught him that homeowners often didn't think to reset their alarms when they were going out for a short period.

He checked the ground floor, but the place was as empty as he had suspected from his surveillance, so he made his way upstairs, past two bedrooms and two bathrooms on the second floor, and then climbed the newly installed staircase to the top floor. He stepped out into an ample space with low ceilings and windows built into the eaves. He looked around. Miss Jenkins had done well for herself to own a house like this, especially if she was the only one living in it.

The top floor was clearly the master suite as there was a huge bed made up with white linen. On one side was an en-suite shower room, and built-in cupboards had been slotted into the space available along one wall, with a large chest of drawers on the other. He was sure this was her room, and the bras and knickers in the top drawer confirmed it. But the best news was the bed. It was made from a solid frame of light pine. Nothing IKEA about this. It was designed with this room in mind, he was quite sure. What he appreciated was the gap underneath. Perfect. He sat on the edge of the bed and waited to hear her coming back, which she did thirty minutes later. By the time Tricia had reached her bedroom, he had slithered out of sight.

He watched her feet come into the room as she sat on the bed to peel off her running gear, tossing it onto the floor before heading to the shower. He had a glimpse of her shapely calves. Then he listened to the shower coming on and carefully eased his way out from under the bed. She couldn't see anything, so he went up to the bathroom entrance. He would wait until the moment she turned the shower off. People seemed to be at their least attentive at that point. He carefully prepared for his next move. She was too athletic for him to make a mistake in subduing her.

40

Roper was working flat out. Every time Hooley glanced over at him, he was staring intently at his screen, his forehead creased in a frown of concentration. He'd been doing that for four hours, and Hooley knew he needed to step in and make sure the younger man took a breather. It was a balancing act — he didn't want to ruin his concentration but was aware that Roper would be all the better for a few minutes away from his research. The pair had discussed this issue a few days ago and Roper had agreed a gentle nudge was helpful. The DCI decided a direct approach was best.

"Jonathan," he called out, loudly. "How about you give me an update and then I buy the coffee?" Roper looked up.

Hooley seized his chance. "Anything new come up?"

"Yoghurt," came the reply.

Hooley sighed. It was clearly going to be one of those days. He would just have to wait until what Roper said caught up with what Roper was thinking.

After almost two minutes of silence — Hooley had been looking at his watch — Roper spoke. "In 2010 the President of Kazakhstan asked his scientists to find a way of allowing him to live longer. He was in his 70s at the time. Two years later, they came back with the idea of a yoghurt drink. They said it could 'improve the quality of life and prolong it'."

"So how come I haven't heard of this before? I could even be tempted myself."

"Because it's not true."

"Oh," said Hooley, who was experiencing the strange feeling that came from drifting between moments of comprehension and incomprehension. He wondered if this was a bit like the early stages of dementia.

Roper was ploughing on. "People have been claiming yoghurt will let you live longer for more than 100 years. In the early 1900s, a leading doctor gave a lecture talking about yoghurt and how it was linked to good gut health. People started thinking yoghurt was a wonder food and family doctors were actually prescribing it as an elixir of life."

"But you're saying there's no evidence that drinking yoghurt makes any difference."

"That's right. The digestive system is incredibly complex, so just eating yoghurt is not going to make a difference."

"OK," said Hooley, anxious to keep this toe hold in the conversation. "So how does this tie into biotechnology?"

Roper gave him one of his slightly impatient looks. "The point is that it may be possible to engineer a new type of yoghurt which could have benefits."

Hooley retaliated with a stern look of his own. "Why do I get the feeling I'm missing something?"

Roper looked at him with a slightly puzzled expression, went back over the conversation and was struck with an insight. "You want me to explain."

"That would be helpful," said Hooley, his face carefully neutral.

"There is something in yoghurt that some scientists have become very interested in. It's a protein called spermidine and, putting it in simple terms, it's supposed to help the cell system to regenerate. In other words, keep the cells healthier for longer."

Hooley wondered what the next surprise would be.

"So, there's a catch?"

"Not exactly a catch, just that there's not enough evidence to say it actually works. At a simple level, the science may be on the right track, but there's plenty more to do. Also, you can't just eat lots of yoghurt and get enough spermidine to have any effect, so it has to be engineered. But it was reading about yoghurt that led me on to some fascinating stuff about living longer."

He stopped talking, picked up his coffee and drained it in one go, a move that made Hooley wince as it was still pretty warm. Apparently untroubled, Roper shuffled in his chair to make himself more comfortable.

"I've never really thought about getting old before. I just sort of assumed it would happen one day. I mean, look at you. You're much older than me, and you'll die before me because that's what happens."

Hooley paused in sipping at his own drink.

"You do recall the conversations we've had about giving people too much personal information? Well, talking to someone about their impending death comes under that category."

Unabashed, Roper pulled out the battered old notebook he carried around with him. He called it his book of "people stuff" and he used it to record observations about social behaviour. As well as being his own reference book, it served as a sort of security blanket. He carefully wrote down what the DCI had just told him and then put the notebook away before continuing.

"Some scientists are starting to challenge the view that nothing can be done to stop you from getting old," he said. "They say we should view ageing as a disease because it takes function away, like your eyesight getting worse or muscles getting weaker. From that, it follows that if we can work out what the disease is, or how it starts, we can find a cure for it or maybe improve function."

Hooley raised one eyebrow. "Well, a cure for old age is something we'd all like to hear about. Especially those of us who are a bit further along the road than others." He studied Roper, but there wasn't even a flicker to show that he understood the mild rebuke. "But how is collecting all this information going to help you focus on the biomedicine companies that have links to Sir James? Also, I don't want to cast doubt on what you're doing, but this is a murder investigation. Don't lose track of the fact we need to identify the people responsible for at least two killings."

Roper was nodding. One of the reasons Hooley liked working with him was the way he handled questions. He didn't get defensive, he just explained what he was doing.

"I won't forget that, but I do think the answers are connected to the research I'm doing now. It comes back to the way Sir James was suddenly killed. He must have discovered something, and most recently he was getting involved in life sciences, so that is why I've been digging around. I'll also need my rainbow spectrum. It's a major field of science and highly complex. I don't think I'd be able to get anywhere without it."

"Have you got anything we can work with yet or something I can get people to start looking into?" Hooley was suddenly anxious to get on; he hadn't realised how much time he had spent watching Roper working.

"Actually, there are two companies I think we should go and have a look at."

Hooley rubbed his hands together in anticipation of getting back on the hunt. A bit of action — that was more like it. He hated sitting around.

41

DF Pharmaceuticals wasn't anything like Hooley had been expecting. He'd fixed the appointment yesterday, and now they were slightly early for the agreed time of 10.30 a.m., which meant he had time to look around. So far, he was disappointed. He'd been hoping for something a bit "sci-fi", with white-coated scientists peering into microscopes and machines with glowing lights and bright displays of information cascading down computer screens. Instead, he and Roper were in an undistinguished glass-clad tower off the Euston Road, close to Great Portland Street and the Portland Hospital for Children. Inside, the double glazing muted the traffic noise to a low rumble. They might have been anywhere. The decor was of the type that looked bought by the yard, with shiny, dark marble flooring and muted colour schemes highlighted by contemporary chandeliers. They approached three black-suited receptionists, arranged in a row behind a high reception desk, the middle one of whom directed them to a row of black leather settees. Through the tinted glass of the windows, they watched the street outside.

On the journey this morning, Hooley had been surprised at what a bright mood Roper was in. He was almost chatty, even offering a brief observation about the weather, which was noticeably humid, rather than his usual exclusive focus on the task ahead. Just as the older man wasn't good at inaction, so Roper became impatient over social interaction. He had once confessed to Hooley that he couldn't see the point of asking people how they were, since everyone always replied they were fine, even if they weren't. The DCI could see his point, and tended to the view of "only speak when you have something worth listening to". This approach meant the pair of them would occasionally go through most of a day without exchanging a word.

Their brief wait ended with the arrival of a man who introduced himself as Mick Jones. He was so fresh-faced he made even Roper look a little ancient. Following his lead, they took the lift to the fourth floor, emerging into a carpeted lobby area. In front of them were security-protected doors, which Jones accessed by swiping a card dangling from a lanyard around his neck. They walked into an open-plan office packed full of desks. To Hooley's continuing disappointment, there were still no machines. Instead, lab-coated men and women sat at every desk, concentrating on their computer screens. Compared to a busy police squad room, the office seemed strangely quiet. No one paid them any attention as their guide waved his arm around the room.

"Our company was founded five years ago and has been doing very well. Under Matt Francis's guidance, we have grown and expanded and have more than thirty people working here. But this is a fast-moving field. New start-ups are being formed all the time, some with just a couple of people.

"Our philosophy," he continued, gesturing them to follow him as he strode past the desks, "is to keep pushing ahead, not recklessly, but to see where we can go while maintaining control. In this field, it can be too easy to make mistakes, so we are constantly checking and rechecking everything we do. That's the process you can see here."

Hooley wasn't sure what he could see and hoped Roper was doing better. As they walked across the room, he saw the younger man was looking around, taking in every single detail.

"Was DF Pharmaceuticals spun out of a university?" Roper asked.

"That's right. David was working on a lung cancer cure while he was at Imperial College. Once it was clear there was potential, he set up the company but kept his links with the university. That way, information, expertise and money gets shared around, which is to everyone's benefit."

Hooley waited for a follow-up question, but Roper seemed happy enough. A short corridor opened onto a large corner office with a view of the BT Tower. Sitting at a desk was a man about Roper's age who they understood to be Matt Francis. He was wearing glasses and was finishing off a telephone conversation, standing up as he ended the call. He was as slender as Roper but a good five inches shorter, and his dark hair was showing the first hints of grey.

They raced through introductions, then Francis was leading them back out of the door. Hooley smiled to himself as he watched the scientist moving with the same air of urgent energy that Roper often displayed, like someone who begrudged the time taken to reach the next destination. They followed a back corridor, finally arriving at more security-controlled doors, behind which was, to Hooley's eyes, something a bit more like it. Francis opened the door and walked in. Roper followed him then stopped so suddenly he might have walked into something.

"What's that smell?" he asked, one hand grabbing the door frame for support and the other pinching his nose with his thumb and forefinger. He went so white that Hooley worried that he might actually be sick.

Francis grinned at him in a knowing way.

"I hadn't realised you were a 'lab virgin' or I would have warned you. I call it the 'cell smell'. As you probably know, a lot of our work needs large amounts of cell material, and it all needs to be stored in appropriate chemicals to keep it in good condition. Some people with a very sensitive sense of smell react as you do, but don't worry, you do get used to it."

Hooley could also detect it now. To him, it smelled part hospital ward and part the odour you got from a crowded squad room on a warm day. Not pleasant, but he could cope. Roper made a visible effort to overcome the odour and entered. Now that he could get closer, Hooley was struck by how scruffy it was. There was a hint of Heath Robinson about one of the constructions, with silver sealant-tape used as binding on rubber tubes that were in turn connected to a variety of battered-looking machines.

"Forget the Hollywood dream lab, all pristine technology," said Francis. "Some of the best work in our field is done by people who create their own devices out of anything they can beg, borrow or steal. What you're looking at here is the work of my best researcher. In fact, she's one of the best in the world in her field of cell regeneration."

Roper looked around and turned to Francis.

"Will we get a chance to meet your researcher?"

The lab boss suddenly looked more serious.

"It's a funny thing, but I haven't seen Tricia since last night. We spoke about you coming, and she was eager to help. It's not like her at all."

42

The moment Francis had revealed his researcher hadn't turned up for work Roper had instantly demanded they leave. Now he and the DCI were outside her home, banging on the door and ringing the bell. Roper bent down to peer through the letterbox.

"I can see a bunch of keys on a shelf in the hallway. Why would keys be inside if she's not there?"

Hooley also looked inside and then shook his head. There were a couple of answers, some better than others.

"We know that she lives alone, so they're not someone else's. It looks like you were right to be worried, which means we need to get in there. I've got a crowbar in the car that should get the front door open."

He returned and handed Roper white protective over-shoes and blue gloves. Then the DCI insisted on knocking again, along with a final call to her phone, before he easily forced the lock.

"Stay close," Hooley ordered as they walked in to begin a careful search of the house. Reaching the top floor, what little hope they had evaporated. Roper walked into the bathroom and picked up a towel that had been dumped on the floor.

"This is quite damp. I'd say she had a shower fairly recently. It may have been this morning or last night."

A frustrated Hooley shook his head at the lack of clues, other than the obvious fact that Tricia Jenkins was missing.

"If it wasn't for the fact that she didn't show up for work this morning, we'd have no grounds for suspicion, but I have to admit you've got me worried now. What made you think there might be something wrong?"

"Do you recall Francis saying that Tricia Jenkins was working on some new theories about cell regeneration?"

He looked doubtful. "I do recall some sort of conversation along those lines, but I didn't take it in properly. If I'm honest, that sort of stuff takes me out of my comfort zone." He didn't add that he relied on the younger man to deal with complex subjects.

Roper explained. "All the companies we found on the computer in Sir James's secret room were looking at different aspects of extending life. One was looking at starfish because they have amazing regeneration properties."

Hooley interrupted. "This helps how?"

"The rainbow spectrum. Matt Francis said Tricia was one of the world's foremost experts on regeneration. When I assigned that information to the rainbow spectrum, I could see there were links to other files I have put in there, including to Sir James Taylor and his murder."

Hooley took a step back, his brow furrowed. "Are you suggesting she had some part in killing him or knew something about it?"

Now it was Roper's turn to look puzzled. "No, not at all. I don't think she's a killer, but we are going to find that her research had something to do with it. I can see that a link exists, but I can't see how. There's another bit of information which backs up what I'm saying. Do you recall that Matt Francis said she was eager to speak to us? Why would she want to do that unless something was troubling her?"

"Even if I was entirely sure what you're talking about, you're asking me to place an awful lot of faith in this rainbow of yours," said Hooley. Roper was about to reply, but the DCI cut him off by reaching out and gently holding his arm. "Let me finish. I'm not saying you're wrong, but it's taking a while for me to understand how you're looking at things." He paused and smiled at Roper. "Not all of us are blessed with a brain the size of a planet, so you're just going to have to put up with those stuck in the slow lane. I like where you're going, but we also need to keep other options in mind. Maybe she's had a row with a boyfriend and couldn't face coming to work." Roper looked dubious, and Hooley held up his hand. "That may not be the best example. I'm just trying to keep all the options open."

He looked around, marshalling his thoughts. "Francis mentioned something about her family having a lot of money, so this might be a kidnapping. You may be right, but until we know for sure, I wouldn't be doing my job if I didn't think about other lines of inquiry."

Roper was looking at him intently. "I'm sure about this, Brian. I think the people we are looking for have taken her because she started asking questions. I also think that Francis has some sort of connection, but I don't know what. Maybe he knows the people behind her disappearance."

Hooley had heard enough and pulled his phone out of his pocket to call the office. "I'll get a team organised, and you can forward that picture of Tricia Jenkins which Francis emailed to you. Once that's done, you and I can get the door-to-door underway, at least until we get some more officers down here. If she was taken from the house — by whomever — then surely someone saw something."

He paused. "I also need a scenes of crime team in the house to see what evidence they can find of anyone else being in there. It doesn't look to me like someone's been clearing up bloodstains, but you never know."

Orders issued, Hooley and Roper began knocking on doors. The first twenty minutes proved frustrating as either no one was home or they hadn't seen anything. They were working their way down the opposite side of the street and reached a house almost facing Tricia's property. The owner, a bearded man in his forties, said he had seen her leaving at about 6 p.m. the previous evening.

"It was a bit after the headlines for the 6 p.m. news. I don't really know her apart from saying hello. She was with a man with a shaved head, and it's the first time I have ever seen her with anyone, so I was sort of surprised for a minute. They got into a blue car, I think it was a Ford, and drove off."

"Did she look worried, or did you get the impression she might have been doing it against her will?" asked Hooley.

The man shook his head. "I only saw them for a moment really, and I couldn't see her face. I think he may have been holding her arm, but I might be wrong."

They left him with a number to call if he remembered anything else. As they walked away, two detectives arrived, and Hooley handed over to them. After briefing them, he added, "I think we can be pretty certain that she was taken, we just don't know why yet or where she's gone. I want to be sure we get every single person who lives here. You may have to wait until tonight when people get back from work. Let me know the moment anything comes up."

43

Julie Mayweather couldn't keep the concern from her face as Hooley and Roper ran through the disappearance of Tricia Jenkins.

"These people must control serious resources," she said. "Their ruthlessness is bad enough, but being able to make so many different moves is equally worrying. And now you're telling me that it's almost certain Miss Jenkins was kidnapped. We all know that kidnapping turns to murder more often than not, especially the longer things go on, and we already know these people are killers."

Hooley's face went darker as he responded. Jenkins reminded him of his own daughter, who also wanted to become a scientific researcher. He was finding the similarities unpleasantly close.

"I managed to speak to her father a short while ago. We'll have a team in place very soon, and we're already monitoring his landline. Still, if they do make contact, I imagine it will be untraceable. He runs his own management consultancy working with banks and blue-chip financial companies, and he's making it clear that he's prepared to meet any financial demands to get his daughter back. I've not got into an argument with him. But there is a psychologist on the way, so hopefully she should be able to explain all the issues to him. I don't want to see him part with money and she still gets killed."

Hooley glanced over at Roper. "But Jonathan is sure this isn't about financial gain. He believes it's to do with some aspect of the work she's involved in."

Mayweather looked at both men in turn. "So why don't we pick up Matt Francis and see what he has to say for himself? He seems a plausible suspect."

"I've been giving that some serious thought," said Hooley. "The problem is we only have Jonathan's rainbow spectrum to go on for the moment. So, I'm wondering if we just put him under surveillance for the moment."

"But doesn't that mean we're taking a terrific risk with Miss Jenkins's safety?" demanded Mayweather.

Hooley held up both hands. "Believe me, I've thought about little else, but Jonathan is adamant that we have a little time. He says that his rainbow spectrum is telling him she's much more valuable alive than dead."

Mayweather studied Roper for a moment. "Is there anything you want to add?"

Roper nodded. "I think we can expect a ransom demand fairly soon. They'll want us to think this is all about money so we can't tell what they're really up to, but actually, they want her for something specific. Maybe she has to recreate an experiment. As I understand it, a big part of this type of work is getting experiments to react the same way every time." He screwed his eyes tight, clearly thinking hard. "What if they think they may need her to make something work properly? It could be they've taken her because they thought they could do something without her but now know that's not possible. She's a leader in a field of work that is totally new."

Mayweather hadn't taken her eyes off him. He was asking them to go out on a limb, and she wanted to be sure he was on top of his game. "Is there any way you can find out what she's working on?"

"I'm not sure," said Roper. "Matt Francis told us this morning that she was involved in such advanced research that he didn't have a complete overview of it. He claimed that if she had to stop and refer upwards at every stage, it would just waste time for them both. They only need to talk when she has something definite — good or bad."

Mayweather steepled her hands in front of her face, clearly deep in concentration. The silence went on for a short while, then she said, "OK, for now we maintain a watching brief. But I want this to be under constant review, and I want eyes on this Matt Francis at all times."

The two men made to leave, but she had news of her own. "I assume you two still have your SAS friends in tow?"

Hooley looked mildly embarrassed. He'd been teased by the rest of the squad over suddenly needing a "babysitter".

"They pick us up from the flat and escort us home again. They're still of the view that no one would try anything while we're here, or even during normal working hours. They reckon the most dangerous time is when we go home. At least it means they're not hanging around us all day."

Mayweather nodded her approval. "Let me know if there's any change in those arrangements. I've also spoken to your wife, and she's prepared to put up with her guards, at least for now. One more thing, the commissioner's agreed to launch a sensitive internal inquiry to see if anyone at the Met has been digging around in your personal files. If there is a mole, I want them found as soon as possible. I'll let you know when we get anything."

44

A loud ping alerted Roper to an email arriving. He glanced at it, then sat up as he took in the subject line. Tricia Jenkins. There was no sender ID. He thought for a moment then opened it. He was confident it wouldn't contain malware since the senders would be more focussed on delivering a message. The IT team would have had quite different ideas, but it was too late; a picture of the missing scientist formed on his screen. Alerted to his sudden intake of breath, Hooley walked over and stared at the photograph.

He leaned down as if getting closer to the screen would make him closer to the missing woman. "They're playing with us, showing us that they're one step ahead. They're saying they know exactly who you are, and they want you to know they have Tricia Jenkins."

He clenched his hands into fists then forced himself to relax; allowing the red mist to rise would just be a distraction. He glanced at Roper, who seemed frozen in place, staring at the picture. The woman was holding a paper showing that day's headline. She was sitting on a chair and staring straight at the camera. She appeared calm and collected, but Hooley thought she must have been terrified. "Do you think there's any chance we can get useful information from the email?"

"I would be very surprised." Roper appeared to drag himself away from the image. "I can't tell anything about the location, she's in an empty room which could be anywhere. I'll get Gary Malone to check it over, but my guess is that this message has been bounced through servers all over the world. We won't get any more information about where it came from."

Hooley was shaking his head. "This is incredibly frustrating, but I suppose it fits with the overall theory that this is all carefully planned to keep us off balance. If we can't even work out what's happened to her, or where she is, we have no chance of getting her back."

Roper looked at his boss. "The fact Tricia is still alive is good news; it shows they haven't been able to get what they want straight away. But it still comes back to how long before they do. For all we know they could be murdering her this very minute."

Hooley couldn't help shuddering. *Someone's just walked over my grave*, his mother used to say.

"We have to find a way to get back into this," he said. "We can't have these people treating life and death as some sort of macabre game of one-upmanship."

"I do have some other news which might help," said Roper. "I spoke to Tricia's assistant this morning, and she's sent over an outline of what Tricia was working on. It's pretty complex, and it will take me a while before I can understand it, but I'm hoping there will be some clues."

Hooley was in the mood to jump on anything but knew he needed to remain calm and not heap unfair pressure onto Roper. "That does sound promising. But it's quite different to what Francis told you. The more we talk about that man, the more I fancy getting him in here for a nice little chat." He pushed himself up from the edge of Roper's desk and looked at the time. "You and I could both do with a coffee, and I take it you'd like something to eat? In the meantime, will you bring Julie up to speed in case she wants to change the plan?"

As he walked out, Hooley couldn't help but wish he had Roper's astonishing capacity to absorb information.

There was an alarming amount of work to get through if they were going to prevent more tragedy. Apart from this new email, he needed an update from the rest of the team to see how the other parts of the investigation were going. With two murders and a kidnap, they were making slow progress. Exhaustive door-to-door at Eaton Square and Putney had failed to throw up any helpful witnesses. They'd been back at different hours of the day, and it was no better.

A mountain of CCTV footage had been accessed and studied, but again it proved of little value. Hooley thought that only Roper seemed to be making progress, but as good as his theories were, that's all they were for the moment — theories. They had no hard evidence pointing them in any direction, and sooner or later that was going to become an issue.

He went to put on his jacket and spotted a copy of that day's *Evening Standard*. He recalled the press team mentioning that the paper was working on some sort of background feature about the inquiry and had promised to leave him a copy. It was always useful to see what the journalists were saying.

The article proved to be a solid piece of work, but the reporter clearly couldn't find any new angle. From the story, it looked as though they had tried to speak to the PC's widow, but she had refused. While Hooley could understand her position, part of him wished she had spoken out; it would have generated publicity, which might have helped. Sighing at his own cynicism, he flicked through the rest of the paper.

"Well, well, well." He spoke so loudly that even Roper looked up expectantly. He apologised for breaking the younger man's concentration and waved the paper at him.

"That strange case of the solicitor who was murdered a while back. It looks like it might have been the secretary who did it. She killed her mother and then committed suicide. For some reason she sent a letter to the paper admitting her role and said it was the only way she could keep her mother safe. This is the first I've heard of it. Someone's going to have to chase that up."

* * *

DCI Hooley headed off, not noticing that Roper had frozen in the characteristic pose that suggested he was thinking furiously. It was the death of the solicitor that was fascinating him, but there was something he couldn't quite put his finger on at the moment. He went back to looking at Tricia Jenkins's current work schedule. He'd come back to the solicitor later.

45

Dan Sykes's Mayfair headquarters had an invaluable asset: a huge two-storey basement that stretched out under the garden. With vehicle access using a garage lift, people could be driven inside without being seen. The first floor of the basement housed a twenty-metre swimming pool, gym, wine cellar and a two-bedroom suite. The lower level offered climate-controlled parking for six large cars as well as what had been described on the plans as storage rooms. In reality, these had been turned into individual holding cells. Each one was highly secure and offered basic bathroom facilities.

One of these was currently home to Tricia Jenkins. In her case, Sykes's instructions left no room for doubt. No harm was to come to her; she was to be made as comfortable as possible and provided with decent food. She was allowed books to read, but nothing that gave her access to any form of news. The intention was to make her feel as isolated from the outside world as possible. Ceiling-mounted cameras allowed him to monitor her. Intrusive but necessary. He liked being able to see her at all times. He preferred his women in make-up, but even though she had none, he thought she looked better than her picture had suggested. Her high cheekbones, generous mouth and large green eyes helped.

Now he was standing outside her door, having spent the previous ten minutes watching her on the link in his office. She had spent most of her time making herself comfortable on the bed while she read a book. At one point, she had stood up and stretched her arms, legs and back. Sykes liked the way she was maintaining her cool. People held prisoner could experience extreme emotions ranging from anger to despair. Tricia had maintained a calm and dignified manner.

He hoped she could keep that up. It made no difference to him whether she lived or died, but he did think it was important to maintain dignity. She was earning his respect to the point where, if the order was given to terminate her, he would take care of it himself. He felt she had earned that consideration. He unlocked the door and stepped inside. He was alone. She might be fit and strong, but she was no match for him. At least not in a fight.

Her bed was a metal cot attached to the wall. She had her back propped against the rear wall while she continued to read one of the books he had provided. Her choice of literature had surprised him. She had opted for detective stories. He wondered if she was hoping that life would imitate art, that at any moment a rugged hero would charge in to rescue her. She finally looked up.

"So, the organ grinder has sent the monkey again. What's the plan now? You start dancing until I can't stand it any longer and reveal all?"

Sykes grinned at her. He did like this woman. "I'm just checking you're OK. Your brain is obviously in good working order. After all, my job is to keep you as happy as possible."

"Letting me go would make me happy," she shot back.

Sykes spread his hands in a mock display of sorrow. "If only I could. But as you rightly point out, I need to keep the organ grinder happy, and he wants you kept here. So, I was wondering if there was some small thing I could do. Perhaps you'd like to choose your food tonight? The chef is excellent and can rustle up anything, within reason."

She made no effort to keep the contempt off her face. "I expect this will come as a surprise to you, but getting kidnapped is doing nothing for my appetite." She paused and then mimed appearing thoughtful, holding her chin as though deep in thought. Then she pointed at the ceiling camera. "Is that thing live?"

He nodded.

"So presumably, you're watching me take showers, even use the loo? I don't suppose I can get you to stop?"

Sykes shook his head and shrugged. Totally unembarrassed. She gave him a disgusted look and picked her book up again. He stood there for a couple of minutes, but she refused to acknowledge him. He decided to break his news to her.

"We may need you to copy some of your lab work for us. My boss will let me know what needs to be done. He's sending over the equipment you might need. Apparently, the other ladies we're holding here will also be useful."

With that, he stepped back and slammed the door shut.

* * *

For the first time, Tricia was unable to hide her fear. The mention of other women made her go cold. Especially the suggestion that they were what she needed to do her lab work.

Suddenly gripped by a desperate need to do something, she threw herself at the door, beating her fists against the cold metal. It was no use. Even if Sykes could hear, he wasn't going to respond. She staggered back to her cot and collapsed weeping, not yet feeling the pain in her damaged, bleeding hands.

46

Barely a mile from where Tricia Jenkins was battling despair, Hooley and Roper were walking towards Buckingham Palace. They had decided to get out for a brief mid-afternoon break. Now they were heading for a small sandwich bar which made superb coffee. It was one of Roper's favourite places, but this time the DCI had almost had to drag him from his desk. Hooley was determined, his sixth sense telling him that events were coming to a head. He might not have a rainbow spectrum, but he did have a lot of experience. From this point, working days would only get longer, and they needed to take breaks while they still could.

Once prised from his desk, Roper was very talkative. He'd set off at a fast pace, but Hooley had gently reeled him in, and now he was walking slowly, eyes on the pavement as he spoke. "It looks like Tricia's work was cutting edge — stuff that no one else is doing, or at least talking about. Fortunately, her notes are comprehensive, so I'm making some sense of it. I think she may have been looking for particular genetic lines to work with, although it's not clear why. It almost feels like something is missing, or maybe she hasn't written it down."

Hooley picked up on the final comment. "Do you think it likely she wouldn't be keeping a full record? From what you've said, she's a very conscientious scientist. Matt Francis may well be holding something back."

Roper suddenly stopped dead, causing the man behind them to swerve to one side. He went off muttering about "bloody muppets". Hooley watched him walk away with narrowed eyes.

Roper had missed the whole thing. "His file fits into most parts of my rainbow spectrum. One way or another, he's connected in lots of different ways to this investigation. On top of that, we know DF Pharmaceuticals is one of the companies that Sir James took a keen interest in. At first, I was thinking it was because they were working on a cancer cure. After his wife died, he supported a lot of promising research, especially for anything that might help with breast cancer. But I'm starting to think it might be some other reason."

He shut his eyes and started gently rocking backwards and forwards on his feet. Hooley had seen him do this before, but he couldn't help feeling self-conscious as they were standing in the middle of a busy pavement. He glanced around, but no one was looking. A woman was heading their way, holding hands with a young boy with Down's Syndrome, and as she passed, she smiled at the DCI and patted his arm. The gesture was so reassuring he went to say something, but she was moving away. He wondered if she thought Roper was his son.

Roper opened his eyes. "The doctor!"

"Doctor who?" Hooley frowned at himself, but Roper had missed the unintentional TV reference.

"I've been thinking about what Sir James's doctor told me when I spoke to him eight days ago. I asked him if Sir James was suffering from any illness at all, and he said these exact words: "nothing that showed up".

"At the time I took that to mean there was nothing wrong with him. But what if he was saying there was a problem, but no one could or would be able to tell? And why would he answer in such a way that it could have two meanings? Everything else he said was very precise. I must have been subconsciously worrying about it all along, but it's only just come back to me."

Hooley knew better than to question this line of reasoning. It wouldn't be the first time Roper had performed this particular conjuring trick. Hooley wished he had a similar ability to pull things from thin air.

He patted Roper on the shoulder. "I think you're right. Let's talk to him again, and this time we can make it a bit more formal."

He nodded back in the direction they had come.

"Much as I hate to turn my back on a great cup of coffee, I think we'd be better off in the office. I need to get hold of your doctor, and you need to try and make sense of what Tricia Jenkins and Matt Francis are working on."

Stepping back into base, they passed Mayweather's door. Hooley glanced in and saw she was on the phone. She spotted him and held up her hand, fingers spread. This was followed by an apparent V for victory sign. He knew what that meant. "You two, my office, five minutes."

She had only just finished her conversation when they walked in and sat down. "I wanted to let you both know that our little mole hunt has produced something," she said.

Both men sat up.

"We found someone in HR who's been tapping into your personnel files. In fact, it's not just you two. It looks like he's been doing this sort of thing for quite a while. His name's Tim Ross, and he lives in Dulwich, South London.

"He's off today, but we have him under surveillance at home and are planning to pull him out in the next hour or so. I'm happy for you to go along. I've told the team commander you'll be there."

Roper was clearly enthusiastic, but Hooley shook his head.

"That's fine if you want to go, Jonathan. In fact, you might well spot something the arrest team miss. But I want to stay here and check on the Francis surveillance team."

Mayweather didn't waste time with any more questions. "In that case, you'd better get going, Jonathan. I assume you're OK on your own. The arrest is being run from Clapham police station, and the man in charge is Chief Inspector Harvey Moore."

She watched him head off and then turned back to Hooley. "Will he be OK down there?"

"He'll be fine," said the DCI. "He's got a specific task to do, and he'll get on and do it."

47

The lights in Tricia Jenkins's cell never switched off, making it impossible to keep track of time. She thought it might have been two days since she had been dumped in here. Her instincts were telling her that she was being held in the centre of London, judging by the traffic noises on the journey here.

She was being tormented by memories of her capture. The man had appeared in her bathroom as if out of thin air, holding a large knife. She had no idea how he had crept up on her, and the fear had stripped her of the ability to react, not even able to scream. The man had stared at her nakedness and then smirked before ordering her to get dressed.

As he led her out of the house, she kept telling herself to run, but it was as though he had her under a spell. He had parked close by and roughly shoved her onto the back seat. She had known her last chance of escape would end when the door slammed shut. Her captor had given that unpleasant smirk again; he had known it too. He had produced a cable tie, which he used to bind her hands together, the plastic biting painfully into her flesh. Then he had placed a bag over her head. It had smelled rank, like stale body odour. She wondered if he had grabbed other women.

He had briefly lifted the bag and pointed at the heavily tinted rear windows before pressing his lips close to her ear, making her stomach churn. He had held her tight to stop her pulling away as he whispered, "No one will be able to see you sitting there, so do yourself a favour and sit nice and quiet."

After that, she was only aware of the constant rumble of traffic. Finally, they had stopped, and there was a sensation of being in a lift before she was bundled from the car and dumped into her cell. The man had removed the hood and cable tie, allowing her to massage the livid red marks on her wrists. After that, the only person she had seen was the one who said his name was Sykes.

She was in a light doze when the door opened, and Sykes stood there. He usually waited for her to say something, but this time was different. He marched in and grabbed her by the hand, pulling her roughly to her feet. Then he spun her around as easily as if she weighed nothing at all and yanked her arm painfully up her back. As she started to cry out, he let her arm go and spun her back to face him.

"You need to come and see something, and I don't want you trying anything silly. That was just to give you a little taste of how painful things could get if you mess about. You can't get away, and nobody is going to come and rescue you, so do as you're told." He grabbed her chin with his right hand and squeezed hard. She couldn't believe how strong he was. She thought he might even be able to break her jaw.

"Do you understand?" Her distress multiplied as she realised how calmly he was behaving. She had no doubt he would hurt her without hesitation. All she could do was nod. She was so terrified she worried she might wet herself.

He walked out of the door, and she followed meekly, her spirit almost broken by this aggressive treatment. He guided her past three more cell doors, all closed, and stopped at the next one, which had its door open. She looked inside to see a white-coated lab assistant, wearing a mask, an incubator with a robotic arm attached for moving trays of test tubes and a lab-quality electron microscope. Then the powerful "cell smell" wafted over her. It was so familiar that it brought tears to her eyes. She was used to it, but some complained it was musty and cloying, almost cheese-like.

As she stood there trying to make sense of what she was looking at, two more men startled her by suddenly pushing past and walking over to the cot, which was covered by a sheet. As she watched transfixed, one of the men pulled the sheet back, and she saw it had been covering the body of a young white woman. The men grabbed the corpse and hauled it out of the cell and over to a parked car, where it was tossed into the boot.

The next thing she knew, she was staring into the blue eyes of a large and very muscular man. There was something about him that made him even more unsettling than Sykes. Her stomach burned with acid, and she wondered if she was about to be murdered. She couldn't imagine anyone would want her to stay alive after seeing that body. She lowered her eyes submissively. As she waited, an image of her mother came into her mind, and this time tears ran down her cheeks.

The man finally lifted her chin and told her to look at him. "I hope you understand how serious we are. The body of that young woman you just saw—" he turned and stared at the car — "She has provided the embryo cells we needed. I want you to make sure that everything is good and that you get the same results here that you were getting in your lab."

He touched her face, but there was nothing tender in it. "It will be much easier for all of us if you co-operate, but if you don't, then I can't afford to waste time. I'm told you're an intelligent woman, so you can guess what happens to you if you don't do as required."

With that, he turned on his heel and left. The two thugs got in the car and drove it onto the lift, which whisked them up out of view. Within moments only Sykes, Tricia and the lab assistant were left.

"I suggest you get on with it," said Sykes. He looked at her pitifully as tears streamed down her face, seeming almost disappointed. He shook his head. "I thought you were stronger than that."

48

Tim Ross had been talkative. But not in a good way. From the moment he had been arrested, he demanded to see his lawyer. Back at Victoria, Hooley had tried to persuade him that co-operating was in his best interests. Ross was having none of it. Anything that sounded like a question was greeted with a firm "no comment". Five minutes of that was enough to convince Hooley he might as well wait for the lawyer to appear.

"Not just any old duty solicitor," Hooley explained to Mayweather. "He's got his very expensive brief coming down from one of those big London firms. The only other thing he's said is to complain about getting injured during the arrest.

"He was in the bath when the boys took his front door off. He says the shock made him spontaneously jump out of the tub and land heavily on the floor, causing minor injury and bruising." He folded his arms, and a mischievous grin flashed across his face before he added. "Personally, I think the real problem was that he was stark naked when the dog unit, a bloody huge Alsatian, ran in and barked his head off. The handler says Mr Ross was attempting to find sanctuary on the ceiling by climbing straight up the wall."

Mayweather suppressed a laugh. They were standing outside an interview room and looking in through the one-way mirror, where a damp-looking Ross was trying to appear dignified in his boxer shorts and T-shirt.

"I've got some proper clothes being brought from his house. If anyone asks, we were concerned that he might be in danger and wanted him out as fast as possible. But actually, I just wanted to mess him around a little bit."

His boss did an outstanding job of failing to hear that last bit. "When are you expecting the lawyer to get here?"

"Any time now, and Jonathan's on his way back." He paused. "That reminds me: we've got Sir James's doctor coming in a bit later this afternoon, about 6 p.m. Jonathan's got a hunch the man was withholding information when he spoke to him at the start of our investigation."

Mayweather's eyebrows rose. She was just about to ask why when a woman appeared dressed entirely in black, from her jacket, knee-length skirt, tights and shoes to the black chopsticks inserted in an X-shape into her dark black hair. Her thick-framed black glasses and round, black earrings completed the look. She was successfully sending out a message of supreme confidence. The DCI tried to estimate her age, but the best he could come up with was between thirty and forty years old.

She looked at him. "You must be Detective Chief Inspector Hooley and Assistant Deputy Commissioner Mayweather." He didn't ask how she knew this or even offer to shake hands, just nodded politely. "Have you charged him with anything yet?" Her gaze, as she made eye contact, was unwavering. She seemed completely unemotional.

Hooley was careful to match her tone, keeping his expression quite neutral. "We're considering a range of offences. At present, he's been arrested on suspicion of committing offences under the Data Protection Act. Still, we also believe he may be involved in conspiracy to assault or even murder. As you know, we can use our discretion as to what information we reveal at this stage. But it's no secret to say we're taking this very seriously." He locked eyes with the lawyer. "I think that will do for the time being, but I'm sure there will be other issues to discuss."

If he had hoped for a reaction, he was disappointed. She shrugged off his words as if he were outlining minor traffic misdemeanours. "I need time alone with my client before I can consent to any questioning."

The DCI opened the door to the interview room with what he hoped was an ironic flourish, only slightly spoiled by the stiffness in his back. "Take as long as you wish."

Watching the lawyer disappear, Hooley turned to his boss. "It's a funny thing, but for all his display of bravado and demanding to see his lawyer, I got a distinct feeling that our Mr Ross is scared. I think he's more frightened of whoever's paid him than he is of us. And that lawyer looks far beyond the pay grade of a little scumbag like him. I think we should look into her background, see if she has any other interesting clients."

Mayweather thought about it for a moment. "I know I don't need to say this, but be very, very careful if you go down that path. We don't need a lawyer like her complaining about police harassment. The commissioner, with his new PR team, is adamant there can be no more high-profile incidents with the Met accused of heavy-handedness and bullying." She looked over the top of her glasses and interrupted the DCI before he could get going. "I know exactly what you're going to say, but that's the way it is for the moment."

49

"So how long was she in there?" Mayweather was as incredulous as her deputy.

"I left her to it, grabbed some water at the cooler, then I virtually collided with her as she was on her way out. She didn't even look at me, let alone say anything. One minute she's all 'my client this and my client that', then the next she's off. That was about half an hour ago. She can't have been here much longer than fifteen minutes."

They were standing in Mayweather's office. She walked round to her chair and sat down, motioning Hooley to grab his usual perch.

"Did they have some sort of argument?"

Hooley shook his head.

"I don't think so. She wasn't in there long enough for a start, and when she came out, she seemed quite calm. I immediately checked Ross, and he was fine. So, no, I don't think it was that."

She was about to say more when a young detective constable appeared in the doorway, careful not to step inside without an invitation. He nodded at Mayweather, his expression serious. "Sorry to interrupt, ma'am, but the DCI said he wanted to know the moment we'd checked the film footage."

He hesitated briefly, looking nervous. "I'm afraid there was no sign of any contact between them. She definitely didn't hand anything to him, and he didn't make contact with her. They didn't even shake hands."

Hooley was careful to mask his disappointment. He didn't want his worry reported back to the troops. He thanked the officer and turned back to his boss. "I didn't have time to shut the cameras off, so I thought we might as well check to make sure she didn't give him anything. There's no audio, though."

"But I presume you'll find a way to talk to her?"

"I think I'll have to," he said, with a small shrug. "But I'm not going to hold my breath. I wish Jonathan were here, I'd love to hear what he made of this."

Hooley was pondering his next move when Roper walked in. Hooley brought him up to speed, and the younger man spent the next five minutes silently running through his thoughts.

Finally, he spoke. "I think her job may have been to deliver a message."

Hooley had been thinking the same thing and was momentarily embarrassed at how pleased he was to reach the same conclusion as Roper. "That's how I'm beginning to see it, but I'd be interested to hear your reasoning." Maybe the way Roper approached things was rubbing off on him.

The younger man interlocked his fingers and then flexed his arms. Hooley winced, he could hear joints crunching. A bit more flexing, then Roper was ready. "Look at the sequence of events. He gets arrested and immediately demands to see this lawyer. Then she turns up in quick time and is gone even faster.

"I was talking to the IT guys down at Ross's house and, from a quick look at his computer, they say he's been accessing all sorts of information. They're going to have no problem making a serious case against him. So maybe Ross knows he's going to prison regardless, and whoever's driving all of this has set up a fall-back plan to make sure he sticks to the script. The best way to do that is by delivering a message."

"Are you suggesting the lawyer was in on this?" asked Hooley.

Another knuckle-crunch. "I don't think so. The message probably only means something to Ross but is otherwise quite innocent. I don't think you would get a top lawyer from a big London firm willing to take a silly risk."

Hooley was on his feet and heading out of the office. "Given that we don't have any audio of their meeting, I think we should find a way to put your theory to Mr Ross right now."

He and Roper marched over to the interview room, where Ross was now fully dressed and enjoying a cup of coffee. He barely looked up as the pair sat down, and Hooley identified himself and Roper for the tape.

"Mr Ross, for the record, could you tell me why you turned down the services of the lawyer you had demanded to see when we arrested you?"

The man didn't bother to look up and instead addressed his drink, which he had placed on the table in front of him. "I changed my mind."

Hooley let the silence build for a moment. "I think she delivered a message."

Ross tensed slightly. It was a blink-and-miss-it moment. But it was enough for Hooley. He stood up and left without another word, followed by Roper.

Outside he turned to the younger man. "Nice work again."

"But he didn't admit anything," said a puzzled Roper.

"Did you notice the way he tensed when I asked him about a message?"

Roper thought back and nodded, he looked crestfallen.

"I didn't realise that was significant."

Hooley placed a sympathetic hand on his shoulder. "These things are complicated, but if you think about it, he's been as cool as a cucumber since we picked him up. That was the first time he's had any real reaction to a question. We need to keep an open mind, but I think he confirmed your suspicion."

As they walked back to their office, Roper sighed. "I don't think I'll ever be able to understand body language."

"Don't beat yourself up over it," said Hooley. "You might not have noticed anything, but it was thanks to you that I was asking the question. I think he gave something away just now, and it proves your instincts were right — as usual. Now, all we've got to do is work out what the message was."

50

Dr Paul Humbert was a small, neat man. He wore a fitted charcoal-grey suit, white shirt, pink tie and black loafers. He was seventy-two years old with thick salt-and-pepper hair that made him look a little younger. He clearly favoured gold: Hooley noted the colour of his spectacles, and his gold-faced watch had a gold and platinum strap. He had a thin gold band on his wedding finger, which Hooley glanced at as they shook hands. He was impressed by the doctor's firm, dry grip.

The DCI and Roper had both come down to meet him after he arrived at the station. They had decided to keep things low-key and talk to the doctor in their office, rather than the more formal setting of an interview room. The DCI had arranged three chairs in a loose circle in front of his desk, and now they all sat down. With a practised flick of his wrists, the doctor revealed half an inch of cuff and his gold cufflinks.

It had been agreed that Hooley would lead the questioning, with Roper jumping in as he saw fit.

"Thanks for coming in Dr Humbert. We just wanted to go back over what you told us about Sir James Taylor. Can I just confirm that you were his personal physician and had been for the last ten years?"

"Correct." For such a petite man, he had a surprisingly deep voice. After a few more questions Hooley decided he was the type of man it was best to be direct with.

"In complex cases like the murder of Sir James, it is important we review the evidence regularly. Now, there is one thing you told my colleague that we wanted to go over again."

The man remained unruffled, but it was clear he was paying close attention, and he nodded once to indicate Hooley should carry on.

"Jonathan was especially interested in a phrase you used when you said there was nothing wrong with Sir James that could be picked up. We wondered if you could help us clarify what you meant."

Dr Humbert sat very still, his hands gently clasped in his lap. He then inclined his head at Roper. "You have a remarkably good memory to recall that much detail, and the truth is you're not the only one who's been thinking about that conversation. I've been going over it in my mind endlessly, and I was a little misleading, but only for the best of reasons."

He let out a small sigh and then carried on. "You need to understand something first. My relationship with James — sorry, I can never think of him as Sir James, much as he deserved the honour — was as much a friendship as a doctor–patient relationship. We had known each other since we were young men. I saw what he went through with his wife and then the selfless way he poured his energy into his charity work. I admired him greatly.

"About 18 months ago, he came to me with a chest infection that he said he had been unable to shift. Although he was no smoker, I was concerned about cancer. To spare the details, test results came back to confirm my worst fears."

For a moment, he faltered, and Hooley knew instinctively that the doctor was recalling the moment. He went on. "James was adamant that he didn't want anyone to know. He wasn't even telling his closest colleagues. Then one day, he came to me in a state of excitement. As you know, a number of the companies he invested in were in the biomedical field. One of them had a new treatment for cancer.

"It wasn't being publicly talked about and hadn't even gone through clinical trials. But by that stage, James was starting to suffer, so he was willing to take a risk. Eight months ago, he began a new course of treatment. He deliberately excluded me because if anything went wrong, he didn't want me associated with it in any way. That's the type of man he was. Always putting others before himself.

"The amazing thing was that the new treatment seemed to work. James had a particularly aggressive form of cancer, yet within three months all the tumours were shrinking back and seemed to be disappearing.

"That's why I said you would not have known he was ill. Normally, treatment for cancer causes all sorts of side effects, not the least being the impact of chemotherapy on the white blood cell count, and the risk of patients getting infections. But he remained fit and well through the treatment. I thought it was little short of a miracle."

He looked directly at Hooley. "The biggest thing I have to say is how much he wanted to keep it quiet. He took the view that it was possible his getting better could go into reverse. He said until he had been in full remission for a year, he didn't want it discussed at all. He only talked about it with me because it was obvious that he was better and he had to tell me something.

"That was one of the last conversations I had with him, and it's why I hedged my answer to you, Mr Roper. I couldn't bring myself to break my promise, but I was pleased when you called me. You needed to know."

Roper had been listening avidly. "This treatment sounds amazing. But you don't know the details about it at all?"

"No. I did ask him repeatedly, but he insisted it had to be totally confidential. He told me that if it worked and after he'd been in remission for long enough, then I would be the first person to know. My job was to monitor his general health, nothing more. I found that very difficult, but he made me give my word that I would not pursue it, and I felt I had no choice but to honour his request."

He stopped for a moment as he looked at both men in turn, then placed his palms down on his legs and puffed out his cheeks.

"When I spoke to Mr Roper, I was still trying to honour my word to my patient — and friend — but afterwards I started to wonder if I should have said something. After all, maybe there's a clue there as to why he was killed."

Hooley took this as his cue to wrap things up. "Thank you. You've made the right decision to tell us, and it may prove helpful. Is there anything else on your mind?"

The doctor pressed his lips together. For the first time, he looked slightly uncertain, then squared his shoulders as though stiffening his resolve. "There is one other thing. After he started the treatment, his mood improved greatly. There was a lightness of spirit I hadn't seen for some time. But then I saw him the week before he disappeared and something was troubling him. I would go as far as to say he was furious about something, and that's not an emotion I was used to seeing from him; he was always so calm and collected."

He took a breath and went on. "I'm afraid I didn't ask him what the problem was. It never crossed my mind that it would be the last time I was ever going to see him. I suppose I just assumed that whatever was troubling him would come out eventually. Since then, I can't tell you how often I've wished I had asked."

51

Ever since Roper had "bullied" him out of his favourite meal, Brian Hooley had been obsessing about returning to the Balti House and ordering a full-fat chicken masala. He let their SAS minders know. The pair were so discreet and unobtrusive that Hooley and Roper often forgot they had them in tow.

It was just after 7 p.m. when the doctor had left, so he decided they might as well head straight to the restaurant and discuss the latest developments over a decent meal. To his relief, Roper didn't raise any fresh health concerns, and a few minutes later they were walking towards Pimlico. Despite it being overcast and a little muggy, both men enjoyed the chance to stretch their legs. Spike had grumbled about them walking the streets, pointing out that it left them vulnerable, but Hooley knew Roper got a lot out of walking and was determined to keep it going.

It was quiet in the restaurant, and they were shown to a corner table. The waiter anticipated Hooley's request for a pint and Roper surprised him by ordering one as well. The DCI studied the menu briefly.

"I know what I'm going to have tonight," he said, rubbing his hands in anticipation. He looked up and saw the beer approaching on a tray, both glasses frosted from the ice-cold beer. He took a moment to admire the drink, then took a long, appreciative sip.

"Quite a day," he said. He was about to go onto the new developments when the waiter appeared and took their order. Hooley kept one eye on Roper as he ordered his usual dish, but to his relief, the younger man seemed content to leave him to it. He really hadn't fancied another lifestyle lecture. As the waiter walked off, he took another pull at his pint and looked at Roper. So far, he'd only taken a sip of his own lager.

He was about to start speaking when his mobile rang. Checking the caller ID, he took the call and listened carefully.

He murmured "yes" a few times, then: "In that case, I think we should put the house under observation. Let's see if we can find out why he finds it so interesting. Thanks, that's good work."

Hooley used his index fingers to perform a drum roll on the table and then double-checked there was no one within listening distance. He leaned towards Roper. "The team we put on Francis," he said, nodding at his phone. "They arrived at Euston just in time to see him leaving. They followed him, and he caught a cab to Mayfair, where he went into a large house, close to Berkeley Square. He was there for about an hour then came back to his lab. Since then, he hasn't moved."

Roper rubbed his chin as he listened. "So that's the place I heard you telling them to put under observation?"

"Exactly," nodded Hooley. "I know there could be any reason why he might go and visit someone, but the office has done a check on the place, and all they can find is that it's owned by an anonymous offshore company. Apparently, there's no way of telling who actually owns it."

Suddenly Roper's eyes were glittering. "In the documents we found at Sir James's home there was mention of a fund that wanted to invest in DF Pharmaceuticals. There was no name, just that it was based offshore. It looked to me as though Sir James was against the offer."

Hooley absentmindedly picked his drink up then put it down again. "That's very interesting. Did it say why he didn't want to take the money?"

"No, it didn't. I suppose it could have been for any reason, but it all seems a bit of coincidence, and I still remember one of the first things you ever told me: 'Jonathan, where you find a coincidence, you will always find trouble.'"

Hooley smiled at him. "If I'm honest, it was my first sergeant who told me that. I guess it's good these things get passed on, and I agree, it is too much of a coincidence. Well, the surveillance will look after itself. We also need to think about Mr Ross and Dr Humbert. What did you make of events today?"

Roper leaned back in his chair, his eyes closed as he checked his thoughts. "First of all, I don't see Ross as being a particularly important player. I think he was given specific tasks but was probably never aware of the bigger picture.

"I placed what we know about him in the rainbow spectrum, and he only has loose connections to a few of the other developments. I remember you once talking about the 'fog of war', and I think he's part of the fog that's stopping us working out what's going on."

He leaned forward, his expression suddenly intense. "But I think what Dr Humbert told us is very, very important. I can fit that information into every file on my spectrum. It supports my theory that Sir James became concerned fairly recently. His cancer treatment fits with what we know about how things suddenly started speeding up. He discovered something he didn't like and that it was related to the treatment he had been having. It also confirms that everything was being done in secret, so no one knew about it, or who was involved in it."

At that moment the waiter appeared to ask if they needed any more drinks, but Hooley waved him away with a tight smile. "Sorry, Jonathan. Carry on."

"We also know that Tricia Jenkins was working on cell regeneration and that DF Pharmaceuticals was originally set up to pursue a possible cancer cure that had been identified by Matt Francis."

Hooley was nodding vigorously. "Even without your rainbow spectrum I was starting to see those links, so let's pursue that for a minute. Have you been able to establish anything about Tricia's work that would help us?"

For a moment, Roper looked frustrated. "Not exactly. As I said before, I still get the feeling that I haven't seen all the work she's done, and I think you're right, that must be down to Matt Francis. I checked with his team, and they said the only person who would have all the information at any one time is him. Mostly they just have the bits that they need to complete experiments and the like.

"The one thing I do know for sure is that she's a world expert on foetal stem cell research. The UK government has been among the first to back that sort of research."

"So, what's foetal stem cell research when it's at home?"

"That's the million-dollar question, literally," said Roper, tapping his finger on the table for emphasis. "The leading scientists tend to keep a lot of things close to their chests. But it's an area of huge interest because that's where they're looking to eliminate diseases through techniques like gene editing."

Hooley held his hand up. "Might be best if you spared me the details. I'll take it as read that you have that in hand. But I assume we're talking about the potential to make an awful lot of money?"

"Billions and billions, I should think," said Roper. Before he could say any more, the waiter arrived with their food.

Hooley watched the various dishes being set out with a benevolent eye. With everything placed, he picked up a spoon and started heaping chicken masala onto his plate.

"Let's eat and then finish our conversation off at the flat. I don't know about you, but I find the more complicated the case, the hungrier I get."

Roper grinned. "I'm always hungry."

52

Tommy Burton had turned up in Mayfair unannounced. It wasn't like him. The man liked to telegraph his comings and goings, a habit Sykes found rather pretentious, as though Burton was some sort of minor royal being announced in the Court Circular. None the less, his unannounced arrival put him on his guard. He knew the only time people changed their habits was when they were worried. He was proved right.

"This man Roper is turning into something of an irritant."

Sykes kept his expression neutral but anticipated being asked to arrange for the investigator to be chopped down to size. And presumably, it would be a more permanent solution than Burton was looking for than last time.

His boss finally stopped pacing. "You need to kill him."

Now he was surprised. Burton had actually used the word "kill". He usually liked to beat about the bush with expressions like "terminate", "remove" or, his favourite, "delete". It was funny how people who killed for a living tried to avoid naming it for what it was.

Sykes braced himself. No matter how he phrased it, Burton was not going to like what he said next.

"There's a problem with that. Every time he's out in the open he has a SAS minder attached to him."

Burton frowned. "I know about that. I thought that was only after work and when they were out on the street. I'm not suggesting you storm their office and take him out, but you can get him at that flat he's sharing with the DCI." He paused for a moment as he thought about something. "Tell you what, since you'll be there anyway, you can do that fucker Hooley as well."

Burton's high-handed manner was beginning to irritate Sykes. He was making it sound like attacking Roper and Hooley would be a walk in the park. It was particularly grating because it was entirely down to him that they knew where Hooley had moved to, which was something that hadn't been acknowledged. He managed to keep the anger off his face.

"I'm afraid there is one other problem. Well, two, actually."

Burton looked at him with narrowed eyes. "Explain."

"The SAS boys have taken to hanging around after they've dropped them back at the flat. They're there all night. It only started a few days ago, so I don't know what triggered it. I only found out because I've been keeping very low-profile tabs on them."

Sykes thought Burton looked suitably surprised at this development.

"I didn't know anything about that."

"There was no reason for me to tell you, until now."

"My sources should have told me that," said Burton, a dark flush rising up his face.

Not for the first time, Sykes wondered where the man got his information from, then he shrugged — need-to-know, and he didn't need to know.

"Just to be clear," Burton continued, "are you saying you can't do the job?"

Sykes clenched his jaw. "I'm not saying no, I am saying it might go very badly. No one should ever plan to go up against the SAS without an excellent plan and outstanding odds. We have neither."

"I thought you were ex-SAS?"

Sykes shrugged. "I was, a decade ago. These boys are current, and current tends to be better. I was pretty good, but I'm not Superman, and I've spent far too much time sitting behind a desk to risk going into a proper battle."

This was a dig at his orders to delegate most of the work. Burton ignored it. "We really do need to get rid of Roper. What about a sniper? That could work, couldn't it?"

"It might," said Sykes. "They tend to walk to work, so it might be possible, if we can find the right spot."

"It needs to be done fast, so don't hang about. In the meantime, anything from the Jenkins woman?"

"I admit I'm way out of my depth on the science involved, but Francis came around yesterday. He reckons the experiment went OK and we should know in the next forty-eight hours or so." He looked at his watch. "Actually, make that about thirty hours now."

"What did he say?" asked Burton.

"Don't ask me for it verbatim, but he reckoned we should know if they've got everything right this time. If that is the case, we can get rid of Jenkins since he won't be needing her again. I assume you'll have no problem with that?"

"Do what you like with her, as far as I am concerned, but just make sure that Francis actually gives you the green light. He's been a slippery little bastard throughout this, and I don't trust him any further than I can throw him."

Sykes nodded. "Don't worry. He might end up with a few lumps and bumps, but I'll make it clear that it's on his word, so he had better not get it wrong."

"Good," said Burton. "I don't mind him getting a bit of a slap. Doesn't hurt to remind him he's part of a team, not the big star he likes to play at his company." He looked around. "It'll be strange to be out of this place, but once you do get confirmation from Francis that everything is OK, I want us to clear out within 48 hours.

"That Roper character has already got far too close for comfort. The more I think about it, the more I want us to focus on getting away." He shook his head in irritation. "In fact, don't waste time on getting a sniper, I'm just indulging my irritation, and we need to think bigger than that. We need to be away."

Sykes noted how it suddenly became about "we", rather than the more usual "me" when things went wrong. He was about to protest, but Burton cut him off impatiently. "I know I raised it, but this isn't about your ability to get the job done. This is about finishing up and collecting our money. Nothing else."

Sykes was at his most Sphinx-like. Burton was rattled and now was not the time to challenge him, but the sniper plan was madness. He would look into it, not because he thought it could happen. He wanted to come up with solid, practical reasons why it shouldn't be attempted.

53

The debate had been intense, but they decided to let Francis loose, at least for now. That could change in a moment. It was Hooley who had argued that he should be brought in for questioning and Mayweather who wanted him left free. All they had at the moment was Roper's theory. A pretty convincing theory, but a theory nonetheless and not supported by evidence that would hold up in court. After much reflection she had decided there was a significant risk they would end up accused of running a "fishing expedition".

But, even with the decision made, the pressure was still on. Everyone could sense that while events were on the move, the details they needed remained frustratingly out of sight. Since his journey out to Mayfair, Francis had remained inside the offices of DF Pharmaceuticals. They had learned he could stay there pretty much full-time as he had access to a small sleeping area. With Tim Ross maintaining his "no comment" routine, it felt as though the investigation was treading water.

Roper had reacted by burying himself in research, and Hooley had gone back to check the rest of his team, gently encouraging people who were working at the limit of their physical and emotional capabilities.

Heading back to his own office, he sat down and realised it was lunchtime. He tried to gain Roper's attention by tossing a screwed-up piece of paper in his direction but there was no response. Hooley rolled his eyes and hauled himself to his feet to cross over and tap Roper on the hand. "I'll get the sandwiches and coffee, then you can tell me what you've been up to."

Roper nodded distractedly, which the DCI took as a yes. Ten minutes later, he was back with the food. Roper grabbed his sandwiches and started eating without saying anything. Hooley, knowing his man, concentrated on cooling his coffee while he waited for his colleague to rejoin the world.

Food finished, Roper carefully folded his wrappers — he liked to create the smallest shape possible — and dropped them into his wastepaper bin. Then he stared at his screen for so long the DCI thought he would have to go and shake him. But before he could do that Roper held up a story he had photocopied from the *Evening Standard*.

"That solicitor you mentioned, David Evans. The one whose secretary seems to have admitted to murdering him. I think he might have something to do with this. Not in a criminal sense, but I think he's connected to the Sir James case."

Hooley was genuinely surprised. This was the last thing he had expected to be told. "What makes you think that?"

"It's a lot of little things," said Roper. "The fact that he was killed at around the same time that Sir James disappeared is one of our 'coincidences'." He mimed quotation marks in the air as he said it.

"Then I couldn't understand why the secretary should kill him. Especially after I read this." He brandished the photocopied news story at Hooley. "The *Standard* has spoken to people who knew them both well. They all said it was a very normal working relationship with no suggestion of a romantic element. It's not just the paper; the same information emerges from the police file.

"It's a real puzzle. I had started out thinking it would be a case of the spurned lover, perhaps because he wouldn't leave his wife, but there's no suggestion of that at all."

He put the cutting down and looked at the picture of Sylvia Gale that the paper had used to accompany the article. "So, that leaves us with the question about why she did it. It made me realise I was missing something important, something I hadn't spotted yet."

Hooley was so drawn in he had moved round to sit on the edge of his desk. "You've got my attention."

Roper leaned forward, his eyes blinking rapidly. "The way she killed him is what's really had me thinking. Where did she get a gun from? I work with the police, and I have no idea of where I would get a weapon from — short of asking you, of course, and you would say no."

Hooley muttered, "I would" under his breath. The idea was not something to dwell on.

Roper was too busy talking to notice. "But it's not just getting the gun. The report says the killing was a single bullet to the head, and no others were fired. That's pretty amazing. I know our SAS protectors talk about "double-taps" as if it's nothing, but my understanding is that getting just one shot right requires some expertise. And a gun expert is the last thing she was."

Hooley thought that was a point well made. The idea of a professional killer masquerading as a personal assistant belonged in the realm of fiction. That left one question though. "Are you saying she didn't do it at all?" he asked. "I thought she confessed all in the letter?"

"There was a bit more in the letter than the paper reported, and she did admit to the murder. That was where I wasted time because I was trying to work out why she did it. But then I realised I was asking the wrong question. The big thing is: who gave her the gun? Once we work that out, we can understand the rest."

Roper paused but clearly had more to say. "There's another thing. Her mother's dementia had been getting much worse. The police discovered that Sylvia Gale was getting worked up over the thought of not being able to care for her. She hated the thought of putting her mother into care.

"But I realised that was another part of the puzzle. If she was so worried about her mum, why wait for a few weeks before killing herself and the old lady? She was running the risk of getting arrested, which would have led to an enforced separation. Her mother would've had to go into care, which is the last thing she wanted."

It was a complicated idea, and Hooley was struggling to get his head around all of it. "I'm still not sure how you're linking this to our case, apart from the coincidence in timing." Then he saw Roper's expression. "Am I right in thinking you've kept the best for last?"

Roper nodded.

"In that case, I want to get the boss involved. We'll go and find her, and you can run it through from the start."

54

"He was a genealogist — a very good one." Roper looked at the two officers. "He was regarded as one of the best people to turn to if you were having problems establishing a family line."

"I haven't been following the case in detail, but I have seen reports, and I don't recall seeing him described as anything but a solicitor," said Mayweather.

"It's not in the police case file, or even in the press coverage. I found out myself from looking at message boards."

Hooley raised an eyebrow, but before he could ask the question, Roper was already explaining.

"I got really interested in genealogy about eighteen months ago. It's absolutely brilliant because you can really lose yourself. Anyway, I thought I recognised his name from some of the online message boards, and I was right.

"He mostly worked on his own, but he got a reputation for offering great advice and being willing to help other people."

Mayweather was intrigued. "So, tell me how you've jumped from bioresearch and missing scientists to genealogy?"

Roper looked abashed. "Ever since I started using my rainbow spectrum, I've been thinking about genetic research, and I wondered what would happen if scientists were looking for a certain genetic marker that was being passed down a

201

family line? Then it came to me. A genealogist might be a good person to ask. From what I've read, David Evans was regarded as the man who could find anyone or any family line.

"I started thinking about the details biotech companies might be looking for, especially if they were trying to find new ways to halt ageing or prevent disease. They would be very keen to have a look at families where people are long-lived. You know those stories: everyone seems to have a ninety-year-old great aunt who smoked forty cigarettes a day and never had a cough, let alone cancer."

Hooley was both fascinated and doubtful. "But surely it would be easy to track people like that?"

Roper shook his head. "That's the thing, though. It can be very hard to find family lines. People change their names, marry, move away, fail to register. And even if one family line had a genetic protection against cancer, they might not have realised it."

Hooley's eyebrows rose at this, but he kept silent as Mayweather looked at him and gave a brief shake of her head.

Roper went on. "If you think about it, there are plenty of ways to die apart from cancer. So, someone might die from heart disease, and no one would ever know that if they had lived long enough, they would never have got cancer.

"All the complications make experts like David Evans important because they can find answers where others fail. Actually, I really wish I could have met him. I think he would have been a very interesting man. Anyway, once I had reasoned this through, I put Evans into the rainbow spectrum, and it was like he plugged in perfectly, linking to all parts of the investigation."

Both officers absorbed all this. Mayweather was the first to respond. "So where do you think this leaves us now? And what should we be doing about it?"

Now Roper looked serious. "There's something I'm starting to get very worried about. If I'm right and they have found a family line, what are they doing about it? Maybe Tricia Jenkins isn't the only person who's been kidnapped."

55

Tricia Jenkins had finally succumbed to despair, laying on her hard bed and sobbingly endlessly. Before long she ran out of energy and curled into a foetal position, not moving at all. Sykes had watched her on the CCTV with a mounting sense of irritation. He was dismayed at how quickly she had gone from calm and collected to a sobbing wreck.

The more he thought about it, the more disappointed he had become. He had believed she was different from most women and had even harboured hopes he might have been able to build a relationship with her. But her behaviour now ensured that would be impossible.

He hadn't realised it, but spending so much time alone he had taken to sulking when he didn't get his own way. That was what he did now. He stared at Jenkins lying on the cot and brooded about the future. He was young and fit and had plenty of money. He was a great catch and could easily start a family. The thought of little Sykeses running around with toy guns made him smile. He could go anywhere. His South American wine venture sounded good, but it was still possible to find parts of the USA that were pretty wild and home to like-minded people.

Without thinking, he poured himself a small measure of scotch. He downed it in one gulp, and the fiery liquid made his nose and eyes run. He shook his head in irritation. He never drank when he was stressed, so what was he playing at now? Could it be from his disappointment at Tricia Jenkins? The thought fuelled his simmering anger against her.

The more he thought about it, the more he decided she might have survived all this if she had only carried on showing the proper attitude. She'd been fine when she arrived, so what was wrong with her now? No one had hurt her. All he'd done was to make the point that she needed to behave. If she'd played up in front of Burton the way she did with him, that would have been the end of her.

In fact, he'd done her a favour — looked after her, made sure she was comfortable and told her what she needed to know. He carried on staring moodily at the CCTV footage, when the germ of an idea hit him. There was a way he could show her how lucky she had been. It didn't come without risk, but it was the only way he could see that might get through to her.

His fantasy that they could be together was the fuel for his actions, and he reasoned he only had the one chance. Now he just needed to focus on the present as he made his way down to the lower basement and opened the door to her cell. She was still curled up on her side, seemingly oblivious. He walked over and gently, but firmly, pulled her to her feet. Her eyes seemed a little unfocussed, so he slapped her face. Not too hard, he thought. Just get her attention. He had to do it three more times before he was satisfied she was paying attention.

"Listen to me," he hissed urgently at her. "You don't know how lucky you are. I'm going to show you something that will make you realise that, and then I need you to get a grip. Things could still work out well; you just have to be strong." He was talking just centimetres from her face. If she hadn't been so withdrawn, his bad breath blasting into her would have made her recoil in distaste.

With that, he pulled her out of the cell and moved down the line of doors to the right. He passed the first door — *not in there*, he thought —and opened the one next to it. A wave of heat and a foul smell washed over them. Inside were six young women dressed in rags and looking close to death. They were lying packed together on the cold, hard floor.

"You see, Tricia? I saved you from all that."

He slammed the door shut, but the stench still lingered. He ignored it and opened the next cell. The odour was just as bad, and inside were three men and a woman. They were older than the women next door, but it was hard to tell how much older. Sykes made sure she had a good look before also slamming this cell shut.

Then he pulled her back to her own cell.

"You see. Just you in here. I made sure no one else was allowed in. That's why you have to respect what I'm doing and realise how grateful you should be. This could all work out very well for you."

She turned towards him and vomited all over his front before collapsing to the floor. He stood there fighting the urge to lash out at her. He knew he couldn't. At least not yet. But he surely would. Oh, yes. She would pay for this.

56

"He's been on the money from the beginning. In fact, this rainbow spectrum thing really is making a difference. Even if I can't quite follow what he's doing, I can see the results." Hooley was parked in his familiar seat in Mayweather's office. She was playing devil's advocate as they ran through what Roper had come up with.

"There's not a shred of evidence to link the death of David Evans to our case. Just total speculation," she said.

"I agree, but it's Roper's speculation. That's worth its weight in gold. I still don't know how he found that hidden room in Sir James's house. That's what led him to DF Pharmaceuticals. Roper's view is that the people who killed Sir James had no idea about the room and panicked when it was discovered because they were worried about what else might have been there."

Mayweather's features tightened. "This is hindsight, I know, but I can't help wishing we'd placed two officers to guard that house. The widow clearly feels I'm to blame, and I can understand her point."

Hooley was sympathetic. "I asked myself the same question. But we certainly had no reason to suspect anything would happen. I just saw it as the normal, boring guard duty. I still don't see why they had to kill him. But these 'people'—" he used his fingers to make air quotes — "are ruthless."

She made eye contact. "Well, we can't go back, that's for sure. So, you were telling me why we should trust Jonathan's instincts on all this."

"There were dozens of companies named in the documents we pulled out of that room, yet he went straight to DF Pharmaceuticals. Just as we get there, it emerges that their top researcher has gone missing, so he was clearly on the right track.

"Sometimes it's easy to think he just gets lucky, but we don't have anyone else in the unit who can make that sort of intuitive jump, certainly not me. He's still going through her material, and I expect we'll have something new soon. As for the link to the solicitor, David Evans, I admit I was dubious at first. But the more I think about it the more plausible it becomes."

He ran a hand through his hair. "There is one other reason, albeit not the most scientific. I can't think of any reason not to support him. If he's right, and they have taken more people than we know about, then I don't think we can risk ignoring him."

Mayweather sounded thoughtful. "The question is just how reliable is this rainbow spectrum of his?"

Hooley shrugged. "It may help if you think of it as his way of explaining what's going through his mind. It's an insight into how he sees things, and that's not something he's been able to do in the past." He stopped and looked at his boss.

She sighed. "I couldn't agree more, but I'd be a liar if I said I was looking forward to spelling this out to the commissioner and his new PR man."

Hooley grinned at her. "High office requires the greatest sacrifice, ma'am." He ducked out before she could throw something at him. When he sat back at his desk, he saw Roper had placed a yellow Post-it note on his screen. It said, "Ask me about the neighbour."

He looked up at Roper, who was staring at him expectantly. "There's a note here that says I should ask you about the neighbour."

Roper needed no more encouragement. "I've just read that David Evans's secretary lived in the same house all her life. It belonged to her parents, and we know the mother still lived there. It turns out the next-door neighbour has been there just as long.

"The police interviewed her at the time of the murder-suicide, but apparently she didn't have much to say. I think we should go back and question her again about the mother. I also think that she needs to see the photos of Dan Sykes and this 'French Pat' character."

57

Mount Street was one of the roads that make up the heart of Mayfair together with Grosvenor Square and Berkeley Square. It also featured two of London's most cherished foodie destinations: Scott's restaurant, a haven of the capital's moneyed classes, and the Mount Street Deli with a host of devoted locals.

The surveillance team sat opposite Sykes's headquarters. It was one of the more sought-after properties and as such commanded a price tag of more than £25 million. The two officers were in the back of a Transit van modified for undercover work. Special panels on the sides allowed them to see out, but no one could see in to spot the camera trained on the front door.

It was tedious work, despite its importance. Since 6.30 a.m. this morning, all they had seen were pedestrians wandering by. Now it was mid-afternoon, and with no activity at the house, one of the pair, Sally Booth, had found a way to pass the time by marvelling at the money on display from the locals. She watched a stick-thin blonde walking past, a bag dangling languidly on her right arm.

"Just look at that one," she said, nudging her partner, Jeremy Woodward.

"If you insist," he replied, his gaze zeroing in on the rear of the woman as she walked past in a pair of tight-fitting, ripped jeans.

"Not her bum, you pervert," said Booth. "Here I am trying to educate you, and you have to immediately lower the tone. No, I'm talking about that handbag of hers. It's made by Hermès. They can cost a couple of grand a go. I've seen pictures in the papers but never actually seen one in the flesh, so to speak. But, since yesterday, I've seen nine. I can't afford the cost of the clothes around here, let alone buy a house."

Even Woodward, who was usually indifferent to fashion, was briefly impressed.

"If I wanted to earn a lot of brownie points, do you think I should get one of those for my wife?"

Booth laughed. "It's not that simple, sunshine. Yes, Brenda would love the bag. But she'd also wonder what you'd been up to, why you were spending so much money on her, and give you a rollicking for spending it in the first place."

Woodward pulled a "you can't win" face and was about to reply when Booth said, "Activity."

He looked up to see a black Range Rover, the rear windows blacked out, pull up outside the house they were observing. A tough-looking guy in a suit jumped out of the front and quickly surveyed the street. Apparently happy, he opened the rear door.

A man stepped out then went straight into the house. Even from this distance, they could tell he was a big man.

"That's not a fella to bump into in a dark alley," said Woodward. "He's well over six feet tall, and did you see the shoulders on him? He's like one of those heavyweight boxers."

Booth wanted to look through the pictures they had taken. "He was so fast, I hope we got something," she said, pushing a button to review the shots. To her disappointment, none of them offered a clear view of the target. She glanced back at the house and saw the Range Rover had moved on. "Let's hope we get him when he comes back out. Hopefully, that car will pull up again to give us a little bit of warning."

The next twenty minutes passed agonisingly slowly, then the Range Rover was there again, and Booth kept her finger on the automatic shutter as the man clambered into the back of the car, which swiftly disappeared into the London traffic.

"We got him that time," said Booth. "Do you want to let them know we're sending something over?"

* * *

The arrival of the pictures sparked a flurry of activity in Victoria. The duty sergeant running the surveillance op was about to send an email when he had second thoughts; he'd go and tell his boss in person. Brian Hooley was an excellent copper, but the digital world left him cold. "Why can't people talk to each other instead of sending pointless messages?" was a constant refrain.

The sergeant grinned as he stood up to walk over to the office the DCI was now sharing with Roper. Before he was suspended, Roper had been in the main squad office and had not proved popular with everyone, although most people recognised he was an effective, even gifted investigator, and he just needed his own space. Sharing with the DCI gave him that. Sticking his head around the door, the sergeant called out. "Pictures from Mount Street, sir. We're running the photo and number plate. I'll let you know the moment we have anything."

Roper had noticed something was going on and came across to look at the photos. After a moment, he declared, "There's something frightening about that man. I bet he enjoys violence. There's also something military about him. He's a man who's used to being obeyed."

"In that case," said Hooley. "I'll get these sent over to Major Phillips, see if any of the SAS boys recognise him."

58

"I can see why they're called 'iceberg' houses," said Hooley. "And how on earth do they get planning permission for digging such a big hole?"

He was looking at plans for the Mount Street property which Roper had been sent by the local planning department. He'd put in a request as soon as he'd learned the house had been visited by Matt Francis. The square footage of the double-depth basement area amounted to the same space as the entire above-ground property.

In response to the DCI's question, Roper stabbed his finger at the plans. "According to the planning office, the council didn't approve such a massive development. They only discovered it six months ago and are demanding answers. They don't know for sure exactly what's down there. At one point, our house, and the ones either side, were owned by the same company, so that might explain how they got the work done with no one complaining."

The DCI could see where this might be heading. "To state the obvious, it seems that the house we're interested in has a secret basement area, and it could be where they're holding Tricia Jenkins. In fact, if your theory is right, they could be holding a lot of people."

Roper nodded. "Everything we know is pointing that way."

Hooley was up on his feet. "I think we need to talk to the boss and suggest she rethinks getting a warrant to raid that place." As he made for the door, he stopped and turned back to Roper. "Was there anything else you wanted to raise?"

Roper looked up. "The house had a massive security refit two years ago. There's blast-proof glass, a reinforced front door and internal doors. The guy at the council said it's a fortress. Apparently, it was claimed that Middle Eastern royalty would be staying there. It seems like the sort of place where that ex-army man Sykes might be lurking."

Hooley shook his head as he absorbed the information. "I suppose this is the price we pay for London being a city that the rich want to live in. Anyway, I'm glad you found out about the security there. It would have been embarrassing if we hadn't been able to get in."

Fifteen minutes later, they were in Mayweather's office, but this time sitting around the conference table with other senior members of the team. Hooley had given the briefing with Roper chipping in. Mayweather noticed that with other people present he'd gone quiet.

The meeting was interrupted by the DCI's mobile. He cut it off with barely a glance and carried on, but a few moments later, a uniformed officer appeared at the door.

"There's a Major Phillips on the phone. He says it's urgent."

Hooley glanced ruefully at his mobile. Presumably, that had been the major just now. He followed the officer to his desk and picked up the phone.

"Tom, Brian here. Sorry to keep you waiting."

"Never mind that," the answer came back fast. "We've got an ID for you on the fella who got out of the Range Rover. His name's Tommy Burton, and he's seriously bad news. Throw in Sykes, and you've got a formidable team."

Hooley rocked back on his feet. "I can't tell you how important that information might be. We were just talking about raiding that house."

The major's voice grew urgent. "If that place has those two connected to it, then you're going to need our help. I'm not trying to top dog anyone, but we have the experience and kit to do this job as safely as possible. It would be a mistake if a police team tried to go in without our support."

Hooley puffed out his cheeks. "When can you get here?"

59

By the time the major arrived, Roper had persuaded his new friend at the planning department to send over the plans for the houses either side of their target property.

"The house on the right is currently empty as it's due to start a major renovation programme next week. The house on the left is also registered to an offshore company, the same as our property. The council isn't certain if anyone is currently in occupation."

"I can answer that," said Hooley. "Our observation teams have seen a middle-aged couple coming and going, so I think we have to assume someone is in there."

With the SAS on board, it was standing room only in Mayweather's office. With Special Forces taking the lead, this was far from a routine Met operation.

Major Phillips had brought his tactical officer with him, and the two men had remained silent while Hooley talked through what they knew. Then it was the SAS men's turn to take over. The major introduced his colleague, Lieutenant Tim Turner.

"I'm going to outline a plan, then it's going to be up to Tim to decide if it's workable. Those crucial details will make the difference." He placed his hands behind his back and went on. "The first thing we need to do is get those neighbours out of the area and discreetly set up an exclusion zone. We don't want a busload of tourists going past as we abseil off the roof. I'd hate to think of all the selfies going up on Facebook just as our boys blasted their way in."

This brought out a low chuckle from the assembled team and helped to ease a little of the tension.

The major carried on. "I suggest we don't need to wait for the green light to start getting things in motion. My team will be there any moment, and they can set up the exclusion area and take care of the neighbours. Once the bosses say yes, we go."

He looked down at the plans that Roper had got hold of and pointed at the roof.

"I think this may be the best way for us to access the building. From what Mr Roper's told us about the work that's been done, we'd have severe problems going through the front door or front windows, at least those on the lower floors.

"However, it seems that the windows to the rear of the property haven't been fortified, so that seems to be our best chance. The only other entrance we might consider is the underground parking bay. Still, we may run into problems if it's well protected. So, I think the rear of the building should be the main focus."

Hooley was impressed by the calm authority of the Special Forces officer. "How soon can you be ready to go, once we get the OK from upstairs?" he asked.

The major looked carefully around the room, making eye contact with all those present.

"Let's just say all the resources we need are close to hand."

This brought knowing smiles from the police officers.

The major clapped his hands together. "OK, let's get on with it. But I would like to say that if anyone thinks of something, please let me or Tim know. We're not supermen, so don't think we won't listen to you."

He looked around again and found Roper.

"Mr Roper, your work has got us this far. Do you have anything to add?"

Hooley could see that Roper was running ideas through his rainbow spectrum. He was uncomfortable being the focus of so much attention, but he needed to answer accurately. After a pause, he finally replied. "I can't say for certain, but there could be several hostages in there, most likely held in the lower basement area. I think they could be in great danger."

The major looked thoughtful.

"Once we get into that building, it will take us a while to get down to the basement areas. That could be life or death for anyone being held there. I think we need to establish how much risk our leaders are willing to take."

Mayweather nodded. "Good point, Major. The commissioner insists on having his new PR man sit in on any further briefings. Apparently, they're anxious to keep a tight lid on this for now. They see this as an opportunity to show the Met is on top of security."

The major pulled a face.

"If there's one lesson I've learned over the years, when PR people get involved, nothing good ever comes out of it. I imagine he'll already be trying to think of reasons why, should something go wrong, it's all down to military stupidity."

60

The surveillance vehicle was acting as the mobile command centre for the operation. Space inside was at a premium, and Roper found himself squashed up against Hooley and one of the communications specialists. Ordinarily, this close proximity to his fellow human beings would have made him jittery, but he was too intently focussed on the video feeds being played out on a set of three large monitors to notice.

Fixed cameras were relaying scenes from the front and back of the house, while more images were coming from the body cameras worn by the SAS and police SWAT teams. The military team was taking the lead, and six troopers, dressed entirely in black, were on the roof of the target property. They had completed their preparations and were now waiting for permission to begin. The major's voice sounded over their intercoms. "Alpha Team. You're good to go on your command in 120 seconds from . . . now."

All eyes were now on the roof as the countdown began. A minute in and Hooley had to nudge Roper; he was pretty sure his younger colleague was holding his breath in anticipation. The last thing he wanted was Roper passing out from lack of oxygen.

After what seemed an age, the SAS team was suddenly in action, seeming to move at an enhanced speed as they abseiled down the back of the building before smashing their way through the top-floor windows and disappearing inside. At the same time, another pair of black-clad Special Forces operatives had dashed up to the gates of the underground car park. They were carefully attaching a small amount of C-4 plastic explosive. The exact amount had been the subject of much vocal debate, with more than one soldier making the observation, "We're only supposed to blow the bloody doors off" — which always drew a smile. This had baffled Roper, despite Hooley trying to explain it was a much-loved line from a Michael Caine film.

Despite the concerns raised in the pre-raid preparation, it was soon apparent that the SAS team was not meeting any of the anticipated resistance inside the house. Instead, they were racing down the internal stairs shouting "clear" as they checked each floor. Following behind them came the police SWAT team, going more slowly and carefully double-checking each floor. It was a big house and offered multiple hiding places, but the property was empty at above-ground level.

The SAS arrived at the ground floor just as the garage doors were blown off. Descending into the basement area they were on full alert, convinced this was where they were going to find the enemy and anybody being held hostage. The live feed from the body cameras showed the steady progress to the depths of the building.

But still, there was no sign of opposition. This made the SAS team leader even more cautious as his men reached the lower basement area. They carefully fanned out around the car park before approaching the area where the six cells were located. The first room was empty, as was the second and third. In the fourth was a young woman lying apparently lifeless on the floor. Even from the less-than-perfect camera images, Hooley could tell it was Tricia Jenkins. A sudden intake of breath by Roper showed he had arrived at the same conclusion.

As they were digesting the distressing images, the search of the house continued, and within minutes the SAS team leader had confirmed there was no one in the property. One of his team had managed to check Tricia and reported she was weak but alive. An SAS medic was racing to help, and Hooley called for an ambulance. He was so angry he slammed his hand on the side of the van.

"How the bloody hell did they manage to escape? We've had eyes on this place for days, and there was no sign of them pulling out. The only person we saw going in and out was that Tommy Burton character."

He suddenly saw that Roper was sat on the pavement holding his head in his hands.

"Jonathan, what's the matter?"

Roper kept his head in his hands. "This is my fault. I must have missed something. But I thought that with my rainbow spectrum I would see everything so easily. If I'd worked it out properly, this would be all over now."

Hooley placed a hand on his shoulder. "Don't give up yet, Jonathan. And I don't accept that this is only about you. We're all on the team, so you mustn't blame yourself. What we need to do now is focus on finding these guys as quickly as possible."

Roper merely remained sitting, his head down. Much as Hooley wanted to stay and help him get over this crisis, he still had a major investigation to run.

"Jonathan, I'll be back as soon as I can, but we need you on this. Don't give up, mate."

61

Roper spent the next ten minutes sitting in silence, wrestling with what had happened, before Major Phillips offered to talk to him. The DCI readily agreed. He remembered the way Roper had been so impressed with the man when he had first visited them. The Special Forces officer sat down next to Roper and after a moment of shared silence started telling him about the mistakes he had made, including two men who had been badly injured. No one, he explained, got it right all the time.

"The thing is, Jonathan, you can sit on your arse and feel sorry for yourself or do something about it. In the end, I realised I owed it to those who were hurt to keep going and do my best to see the job through. You can't just let go."

Roper carried on sitting there for a while longer and then looked up. "You're saying it's selfish of me to blame myself because it's making me stop working on the case, and that's not going to help anyone." He ran his fingers through his hair and let out a deep breath. "I understand. If I stop now, I'm making it about me, and that's not what I want at all."

Hooley stifled a little cheer as he watched on. Roper was back on the hunt. He patted both men on the shoulder and quietly admitted that while he was pleased that the major had found a way to get through, he did wish he'd been able to do it himself.

But there was no time for that, and they needed to crack on. He wanted Roper in that basement straight away. It was clear from a closer examination of the "cells" in the lower basement levels that a lot of people had been kept in them. There was also some medical equipment, some of it similar to what they had seen at DF Pharmaceuticals.

He followed Roper into the basement level, where he spent almost an hour slowly working his way around the area, occasionally shouting out or tapping at the walls. Hooley was torn between wanting him to move faster and knowing he had to be left to work at his own pace. He did have to stop himself grinding his teeth in impatience.

Finally, Roper reached the cells, pausing outside before entering and carefully examining each room. At the third door, he recoiled as though he had been hit by something.

"I can clearly smell traces of sweat, blood and faeces in this one. It's in the others too, but much stronger in this one."

Hooley stepped up and sniffed cautiously. He caught an unpleasant undertone but was unable to say what the smell was. Meanwhile, Roper had been taking a series of breaths, and then he inhaled deeply and walked into the cell. He tapped the rear wall, cocked his head and stared at it. He was so absorbed he started breathing normally. He pressed both hands on the left-hand side of the wall, about halfway down. It slid silently back to reveal a dark passage.

"This is how they got out. I bet you anything this passage leads out through the house at the back of this one. Another thing I should have thought about."

Hooley noticed Roper's expression. It was something he had never seen before. Roper was furious. Maybe now he'd do something about catching up with the bad guys.

"I want to get back to the office and start really looking at my rainbow spectrum. The answer is going to be there, I'm just not looking in the right place yet."

62

Hooley's request that the David Evans team re-interview Sylvia Gale's neighbour had brought swift results. Judging by the email report, Roper had been on the right track. Two detectives had spoken to the neighbour, who said there had been an unusual episode with the mother. About six months earlier, she had managed to get out of the house and disappear, something which had never happened before. The neighbour said Sylvia had been frantic with worry, until she received a phone call from the security office at a shopping centre in Bromley, a town to the south of Beckenham. Security guards had found her clearly confused mother wandering around in her nightgown. In her hand, she had a piece of paper with the name Sylvia Gale on it, and what proved to be her telephone number.

Sylvia had dashed to the centre to collect her, and in her relief the neighbour said she hadn't thought to question what had happened. It was only later that she started to think about how strange it had been. She couldn't understand how the mother had got out of the house, since it had been extra secure following her dementia diagnosis. Plus, there was the question of how she had made it to Bromley. It was too far for a frail old lady to go there on her own.

When she had tried to raise the issue, Sylvia was evasive. She made out that her mother must have remembered going there when she was well and had re-created the journey. It was well known, said Sylvia, that dementia sufferers have a brilliant recall of events in the distant past. The neighbour had let it go. She assumed Sylvia didn't want to talk about it because she felt guilty over what had happened.

Roper looked up from reading the document. "It seems pretty obvious they took the old lady to warn Sylvia Gale what might happen if she didn't do what they asked. They must have thought it was perfect. The woman they had monitoring David Evans was under their control. They had found the only way they could effectively undermine her loyalty to him.

"That must have been how they persuaded her to shoot him. They probably told her that next time her mother would be dumped all alone in the middle of some woods, or similar."

Hooley nodded but did have a concern. "Why not just bump Evans off themselves? After all, we know they're not squeamish when it comes to murder."

Roper looked serious. "I think it's because they're cruel and controlling people who enjoy manipulating others into doing terrible things. Like the sort of bullies you get at school who don't know when to stop."

Hooley noted the set expression on Roper's face. His observations were clearly based on personal experience. He hoped the younger man wasn't reading too much into it but took comfort from the fact that Roper had been proven right with even bigger intuitive jumps.

63

Dan Sykes was sitting in a grubby white van watching members of his "old team" execute a text-book entrance into the Mount Street house. But he knew they were going to be disappointed and had stayed behind because he wanted to be close by when they realised they were too late. Parked well outside the 300-metre exclusion zone, he'd found a spot where his powerful binoculars gave him a close-up view of the action. The bang when they detonated the C-4 was seriously loud, generating a cloud of dust and sending the plump pigeons of Mayfair flapping madly into the sky.

Despite what he'd said to Tommy Burton about not being a match in a straight fight with current SAS operatives, his ego meant he still backed himself. He had kept in good shape and was more than a match for most opponents. Watching what was going on gave him a rush and fed his sense of superiority. He calculated it was a risk well worth taking, given there was only a slim chance he could be caught.

As he watched, he thought he had to hand it to Burton. The man had delivered the warning in plenty of time for them to get out of the house. Yet again Burton had proved he was formidably well connected when it came to getting inside information. In truth he was a little envious but cheered himself up as he imagined how frustrated the police and SAS troopers were going to be. His sense of triumph had led him to linger longer than he had originally planned as he couldn't resist the sense that he was defying the odds.

One of the best moments had come when he had seen a clearly frustrated DCI Hooley emerge from the surveillance van and slam the side door in obvious frustration. That must have been the very second he learned they were too late. They would have found Tricia Jenkins by now, as he had made the decision to leave her behind, what was left of her. Right at the end, she'd surprised him by showing some of her earlier spirit. Too late of course, but she had put up a fight. He had the scars to show where she had dug her nails into him. But her resistance soon faded, and he had given her a beating for her trouble. As far as he was concerned, he'd left her for dead.

He checked his watch. He'd been there for more than an hour. It really was time to go. He was just reaching for the ignition key when there was a loud tap on his side window. Standing on the pavement were two black-clad troopers. An expert on guns, he realised exactly what weapons they were carrying. One was holding an MC51 short-barrelled assault rifle, loaded with 7.52 mm ammo, and the other had a Remington 870 12-gauge pump-action shotgun. There were lots of arguments about the relative merits of both weapons, and many claimed there were superior alternatives. Sykes wasn't too bothered about that right now. He knew that in the hands of experts and used at close range, he would be reduced to mincemeat. He slowly raised his hands in the air.

The door opened, and none too gently he was dragged from his seat and pressed down face first on the cold pavement. To his disgust, he had a close-up view of a squashed dog turd, but his captors seemed unsympathetic to his plight. His hands were swiftly tied behind his back with zip ties, yanked tight enough to pose a risk of circulation problems in the not-too-distant future. Then he was frog-marched back to the house.

Sykes was dumped on the floor of what had been his office and left to struggle up to a sitting position as best he could. It was all part of a softening-up process he knew had started from the moment he was grabbed. Finally, managing to sit up, he studied the two guards in the room with him. These two both had MC51s, which they were holding in the approved position, ready to fire in an instant.

Their faces were obscured by black balaclavas, and neither said anything. He tried to get a conversation going by asking for water, but he might as well have been talking to himself for the effect it had. His guards studiously ignored him. This went on for another ten minutes, then a man walked in who he recognised, Major Tom Phillips.

He grinned with his best cheeky-chappie expression. "Tom Phillips, as I live and breathe. What a joy to see a friendly—" His words were cut off as the major lifted a booted foot and placed it firmly in Sykes's chest before forcing him down on the carpet. The pressure was immense, and he found himself struggling for breath. Then it was released.

"Stop pissing about, Sykes. You've already made one big mistake by hanging around. Did you forget the bit in the manual that says we always check outside exclusion zones? It's amazing how often you 'criminal geniuses' can't seem to stay away. I suppose you wanted to gloat over escaping. Well, gloat on this." He delivered a vicious punch to Sykes's left kidney, which nearly made him throw up.

The major knelt down and spoke just inches away from Sykes's face. "I hate little scumbags like you. If it was down to me, I'd have put you down back at the van. We might have managed to scoop up enough to put what was left of you into a plastic bag and post it to your old mum — assuming she'd want you."

To Sykes's complete surprise, the major then stood up and walked out of the room. He was sure he was about to be offered a deal in return for his "co-operation". He could only stare at the door with his mouth open. He stayed on his back, assuming that any attempt to move would have him forced back to the ground. But time passed, and he realised that they must be playing by different rules. He managed to get back into a sitting position and tried to ignore his throbbing wrists and burning kidneys.

He put himself into a light trance. Twenty minutes later the major was back, and Sykes decided it was time to open negotiations. "I expect by now you've discovered that the pointy-headed Matt Francis has disappeared. So, if you want to know anything about our operation, you're going to have to talk to me."

Major Phillips tensed. He was right, then. They didn't have anyone else. He stopped talking for a moment as he allowed an unpleasant sneer to appear. "If you want to save some lives, you're going to have to offer me a deal."

At no stage did Sykes suffer the slightest doubt or introspection about being held. Since his release from the Syrian prison, where he was sure he would die, he had formed the view that he had a guardian angel who would make sure he always came up smelling of roses — no matter how grim the odds.

64

"How can we possibly do a deal with someone when we've got him on CCTV murdering a policeman? This is madness." In the face of Hooley's outburst, Mayweather maintained an enigmatic expression. While she had every sympathy with her deputy, he needed to get over his anger as quickly as possible. The decision had come straight from the top, and her attempt to argue against it had been firmly knocked back. Now they were going to have to get on with it.

"It's no more appealing to me than it is to you, but the idea came from the new PR man. He says that if it came out that we allowed innocent members of the public to die when we could have done a deal, then it will be damaging. We'll be seen as more bothered about ourselves than the people we're meant to protect. The commissioner was in complete agreement. No one is talking about letting him go free, we just offer him the chance of a slightly easier ride through the system if he helps us."

While Hooley understood there was no way around this order, a part of him refused to go down without a fight. "I just don't understand how these people can start playing politics at a time like this. It's almost as though they don't care about catching the bad guys so long as it plays out nicely on Twitter."

Mayweather looked at Roper. "What do you think, Jonathan?"

Roper didn't pause. "I can see the PR argument very clearly. Our colleague is already dead, and that's terrible for his family and friends, but there's nothing we can do to bring him back. At the same time, I believe the other victims are still being held hostage. It would look very bad if they died because we refused to do anything at all. So long as Sykes goes to prison, then it balances out."

Hooley grimaced. He knew Roper was talking sense, but he couldn't help imagining how the PC's widow would react if she was sitting in on the discussion. The problem was he couldn't come up with a better idea. If you stripped the emotion out of it, as Roper had just done, the answer was clear. "I guess you're saying we have no choice — unless that rainbow spectrum of yours is about to save the day again?"

His hopes, slight as they were, were instantly dashed. "I've got nothing. I'm sure I'm missing some critical detail, but I've no idea what it might be. My big hope is that once you start talking to Sykes, he'll provide new information that I can plug in and get some more answers.

"But there's a big problem. Looking at everything that we have now, I'm sure the gang is still in the process of shutting down their operation. So, I expect Sykes will be perfectly happy to sit tight and waste time, no matter what he's offered.

"These people have shown they're totally ruthless, so Sykes won't be bothered if any more victims die. In fact, my guess is that he'll have no concerns about going to prison. Partly because he's a very tough man and partly because he's banking on being rescued by his military contacts."

Major Phillips had been standing at the back listening and now stepped forward. "I think that last point is well made. We have no idea where Tommy Burton is, and he'd think nothing of launching an armed assault on a prison."

Mayweather looked as concerned as Hooley could ever remember seeing her. "Clearly, this is going to be very difficult, but we have to make the victims our top priority. I know this is hard for all of us, but Jonathan is right; we must assume there are people alive who need our help."

Roper looked around the room. "I've identified some topics that I believe Sykes will be willing to talk about, including the murder of David Evans and the murder-suicide of Sylvia Gale and her mother. I was reading the background briefing on Sykes provided by Major Phillips. There's a detailed account by a psychiatrist who interviewed him a year before he vanished from the SAS. He'd already been spotted as a potential problem, and they were anxious to find out what made him tick. He said Sykes was a true narcissist, someone who's obsessed with himself and believes he's far more intelligent than anyone else. That, coupled with a streak of sociopathic tendencies, makes him 'potentially a very dangerous man', according to the psychiatrist."

He broke off for a moment as he trawled his memory, something Hooley recognised from the way his gaze had switched to the middle distance. For that brief period, he was unaware of how he had grabbed the undivided attention of the rest of the team.

"My estimation, from studying the files, is that he can be prompted to tell us about the murder of David Evans and the murder-suicide of Sylvia Gale and her mother. It took us weeks to find that connection, and he'll be pleased with himself over that. The fact that they were able to manipulate Sylvia Gale to kill her boss will have especially delighted him. Plus, he'll view it as a safe topic because he won't be giving away any information about what they've done with the hostages."

Hooley was the first to respond. "As usual, your attention to detail is extraordinary. I didn't even realise we had a psychiatric report on Sykes."

He looked at the major, who shrugged an apology. "With everything else going on, it slipped my mind. To be honest, it was done a long time ago — before I was promoted to major. I just assumed it was a routine psych evaluation. We all have to undergo them from time to time."

"Well, not for the first time, we're grateful to you, Jonathan," said Hooley. "But I'd still like to start the interrogation by asking him the direct questions first. If there's any chance of getting a quick response, then we have to explore it. I say we put the deal on the table and see what response we get. If he plays hard to get, we go down the path that you've identified."

Roper was leaning against the wall, staring down at the floor. "It won't hurt to do what you say, but don't be disappointed when he plays up. I've been able to build up a detailed picture of our man, and my reading of the situation says Sykes will play for time." He fidgeted with his tie for a moment then carried on. "There is another aspect we all need to be aware of. Their biotechnology research is clearly advanced beyond pretty much anything else out there. We already know they have some sort of cancer therapy that halts the disease. But if they're making progress on finding a way to extend life, then it will be the most valuable medical breakthrough yet.

"It would be worth enormous amounts of money. It's not an exaggeration to say that whoever comes up with a way of allowing us to live longer will earn billions. And if you add in a cancer cure as well, then make that trillions. Because we don't have Matt Francis, we have to assume they have the ability to go away and start up in a country like North Korea. That means it's in Sykes's best interest to keep quiet, since I'm sure he'll have been promised a big pay out. I've been looking at it through the rainbow spectrum, and it seems clear to me there is a very cold mind at work who we haven't yet identified. I don't believe it's Tommy Burton — the files say he's like Sykes, an action man. We still need to find the planner behind all of this."

Mayweather was nodding in agreement. "I share your frustration over Matt Francis being on the loose. I'm sure Sykes is going to prove a formidable opponent. But I do have some good news. We picked up a lot of the scientists from DF Pharmaceuticals, and we have Francis's assistant, Mick Jones.

"He may have some invaluable information for us. I've got a team ready to start questioning him, then you two—" she glanced at Hooley and Roper — "can have a go at him later."

65

With Sykes flagged as a significant escape risk, security at Victoria was higher than anyone could remember. The plan was to eventually move him to the high-security police station at Paddington Green, but that was currently full of people picked up in an anti-terror sweep. So Victoria had become like a fortress. There were armed officers at every point of entry, and Major Phillips was providing advice and support, along with some of his men. Much attention was focussed on the fourth floor, where Sykes was being held, and Hooley was leading the questioning. After Roper's sobering appraisal of what they faced, he was being careful to keep his emotions firmly in check.

The DCI and Roper sat in a bland interview room, just big enough for a large wooden table with functional wooden chairs either side. Sykes, who had been loaned a clean white T-shirt to replace his own filthy one, was sitting on one side, staring knowingly at the oblong one-way mirror on the opposite wall. There was a plastic bottle of water in reach of his right hand, but he hadn't touched a drop. High up on the walls were a pair of cameras that could, between them, cover the entire room, and a small recording device. Hooley was firing out questions.

He had only got as far as the third question before it became clear Roper's analysis had totally nailed it. What Hooley hadn't anticipated was that being pre-warned meant he was able to remain calm in the face of Sykes's stalling tactics and antagonistic behaviour. It stopped him gaining the upper hand, but it was only a small victory. It didn't make any difference to the biggest problem; the mercenary was flatly refusing to give anything away.

Sykes was leaning back in his chair, tapping the side of his nose. "The way I see things, I've got all the time in the world. There's no chance you're going to let me walk out of here, so it's all about what you can do for me. But I'll let you into a little secret." He leaned forward, all pantomime villain. "I never rush into things."

He leaned back again. "For example, if I'm in a restaurant, I like to study the whole menu very carefully before I make a choice. I'd hate to miss out on some little gems because I didn't take my time. So, you're going to have to bear that in mind before I can even think about telling you what you seem so anxious to know." He paused for a moment, then affected boredom. "That's assuming I know the answer to your questions at all."

Mayweather and Major Phillips, who were observing through the one-way mirror, both clenched their fists as they listened to what he was saying. "Roper was right," the major said. "Look at him; he's almost preening with his own self-importance. Back in the day, he had a reputation as a smarmy sod, and it seems nothing has changed. Right now, I could happily choke the little bastard."

Back in the interview room, while he had remained calm up to now, Hooley knew that much more of this behaviour was going to get under his skin. He glanced at Roper and then had an idea about how he might be able to exert some pressure of his own. It was a gamble, but one he felt worth taking if it got them the answers they badly needed.

"I won't insult you by saying you can help yourself by helping us. You're going to prison for a long, long time. But you need to bear in mind that, thanks to Jonathan, we're one step ahead of you. He's already calculated that you're hoping to get busted out.

"I hate to disappoint you, but there are prisons, and then there are *prisons*. We can pursue you under anti-terrorism legislation, and that means you could end up in a black site in a very deep hole where no one will ever find you."

He resisted the urge to say anything as he watched an uncertain expression flash across Sykes's face. "Oh, I suppose you thought only the Yanks had black sites. Well, dummy, what would be the point of a black site if everyone knew about them?"

With that, he tapped Roper on the arm, and the pair of them walked out. The waiting Mayweather said, "Black sites? Where did that come from?"

Hooley shrugged. "It could be true."

They decided to leave Sykes alone for a short while, which gave Hooley the chance to swallow a cup of tea before the second round.

It had been agreed that this time they would fall back on Roper's list of questions, and Hooley noted the way that Sykes appeared to become a little more relaxed at this line of inquiry. A short while later he was boasting about what had happened to David Evans.

"I'm afraid that in every campaign there will be casualties, and that's what happened to him. In a way, it was his own fault. He started asking too many questions, so we had to shut him up.

"That soppy bird who was his PA was obsessed with her mother, so it was easy enough to put pressure on her. I just took the gun round to her house when it was time, showed her how to point and fire it, and then left her to it.

"We had quite a chat between us about the best weapon she should use, and the final choice was my idea, and a very good one it was too. It allowed her to do the job perfectly." That smug expression appeared on his face once again.

Hooley thought that, in many respects, this casual indifference to forcing innocent people into impossible situations was the most sickening thing he had heard Sykes say yet. It was the way he was so dismissive. He realised he was grinding his teeth with the effort to keep his temper in check. Needing to keep things moving along, he asked why they had recruited a genealogist.

Sykes looked at him for a moment, clearly making some sort of calculation. "I don't suppose it matters if I give you the outline; there's no way you can find out anything else. We needed to find current members of a family with a history of immunity to cancer. The twist was that they hadn't realised it.

"We had information that identified this family from mid-Victorian times. They were famous because, it was claimed, that they were long-lived owing to a special potion they drank. They used to appear at stage shows all over the country to promote its benefits. It wasn't true, at least not the elixir bit, but they believed it, and that's what made them so convincing. But the real joke was that their genetic line really was unique.

"We had the name of the original family, but by the twentieth century, the direct line had vanished and was proving impossible to track down. We turned to Evans to see if he could help us.

"It took him months, but he finally found the people we needed. After that, it was my job to round them up and make them offers they couldn't refuse. Then they were put to use in the research being done by old pointy-head. Some garbage about living forever, apparently."

Sykes paused and looked smug. "I don't suppose you hear many a tale like this. It was a lot more interesting than some of the work I've done. The pay and perks have been especially good." With that, he gave Hooley a lewd wink and sat back in his chair.

"So, what happened to them?"

Sykes looked over at the mirror then gave a little wave. Mayweather flinched, then caught herself. The former SAS man jutted his chin at the window, and Mayweather shook her head. "That's a little trick he learned in Hereford. It's supposed to help give you a feeling of being in control, but I don't suppose the prat needs much help with that."

Inside the interview room, Sykes was pointing at the mirror. "I suppose your fragrant lady boss is here. Tell you what, just because she's taking such an interest, I'll give you a little bit more information. Those people from the family tree — well, once we got what we needed, there was no more use for them. So, I had to make sure no one else would be able to get anything from them."

Hooley decided now was the time to take another break. It was that or punch Sykes.

66

As Roper pulled the door shut, Hooley stretched his arms out to try to ease some of the tension he could feel building in his neck. To his dismay, he was treated to the sound of his elbow joints crunching loudly and a pain stabbing through his left shoulder. *This interrogation is making me grow older by the minute*, he thought gloomily.

Mayweather was looking visibly angry, and he raised a quizzical eyebrow. She responded by pulling the three of them further down the corridor as if to get away from the toxic Sykes, now sitting alone in the interview room. They were joined by the duty sergeant, Geoff Purbeck, who had the key job of being on top of all developments coming from suspects in the interview rooms.

"Tell them, Geoff. But start from the beginning," said Mayweather. Her expression grim.

Out of habit, the uniformed officer checked there was no one listening nearby. "As you know, we started talking to Mick Jones a short while ago, while the DCI and Mr Roper were talking to Sykes. Anyway, Jones didn't need any prodding. He's been spilling his guts from the moment he sat down, and we have it all on the tape."

For a brief moment, he managed to look both pleased and worried, then he carried on. "I just want to warn you now that what he's been telling us is pretty bad. He said Matt Francis and Tricia Jenkins have been making some amazing medical breakthroughs, especially in cancer treatment. Still, it's how they got there that's the problem.

"At first, says Jones, everything seemed fine — the results of groundbreaking science. They were taking cells from embryos that were just a few days old. Apparently, the UK is one of the leading nations in this type of work, something to do with government legislation being relaxed.

"But Jones says Matt Francis was harvesting the cells in the worst way possible, and that's where Sykes comes into it. He's been trafficking young women into the country and picking out the healthiest and prettiest ones to be forced into the programme. Then they're raped until they become pregnant, and the women are made to keep the baby so that cells can be extracted at different stages of the pregnancy. As far as Francis and Sykes were concerned, the women were treated as though they were 'grow bags for cells'. A lot of them died because they were treated so badly. And Francis was behind it all. He had a theory that he needed a huge variety of cells from different women and at various stages of pregnancy so that he could judge which was the most effective."

There was a shocked silence at this news. Hooley said, "Did Jones offer any information about exactly how many women are involved? And why rape them?"

Purbeck threw his hands in the air. "To answer the first part of your question, it's not clear to me how many, just a lot. Jones is saying that he'd only just found out about it and was being threatened by Sykes. He's claiming that Sykes was treating the rape of these women as a perk for him and his men.

"He says it's been going on for ages. The women were picked up from refugee camps all over Europe. Jones is claiming that when he confronted Francis, he was told to think of all the good they were doing with inventing new drugs. Then Sykes turned up and threatened to kill him. Again, according to Jones, his boss apparently said they could never have found the cancer cure without the different stem cells."

Roper looked thoughtful, and Hooley knew he was too caught up in the details of the investigation for him to react to the horrific treatment of the women that Purbeck had just described. Then Roper did a little half-nod as if confirming some thought. "This does fill in the gaps. I just need a little more time on my own, and then I think I might be able to work it out."

With that, he walked off. Mayweather was about to call out, but Hooley laid a hand on her arm. "Leave him be. Hopefully, he'll be back with more answers."

67

Roper took the stairs up to the fifth floor and closed the office door behind him. He badly needed this time alone and wanted to shut the world out as he pulled together the final threads of the investigation. He picked up a handful of printer paper, sat at his desk and started to slow his breathing as he put himself into a trance. Conventional methods to do this include focussing on a favourite space or imagining the perfect, sun-kissed beach. Roper had an approach that was all his own.

He drew on an image of his heart valves opening and closing. By focussing hard enough, he could slow them down. He'd once told Hooley about it, but the DCI had been horrified. He'd warned him he could stop his heart altogether. Roper hadn't been deterred. He carried on with his method but kept the details to himself. Especially since, on a couple of occasions, he'd made himself pass out.

But now there was no time for worrying about that. As he gently slowed his heart, he carefully counted out two stacks of twenty sheets of paper. Then he began gently flapping each handful. It intensified his sense of serenity. Over the years, he had tinkered with his approach and was confident that twenty sheets in each hand was just the right amount to achieve the effect he was hoping for. The weight of paper produced a feeling of resistance that he could feel in his fingertips. He also enjoyed the gentle sensation of a breeze caressing his face as he flapped backwards and forwards.

Ready for the next step, he leaned back in his chair and imagined himself sitting in his childhood bedroom. Growing up, this had been a place of sanctuary where he could flee the pressures of school.

He shoved these memories aside, and his thoughts went into super-slow motion. Now he could introduce the rainbow spectrum and examine everything they had learned up to this point. Had anyone walked in at that point they would have been treated to the sight of Roper leaning right back, seemingly about to topple out of his chair as he went deeper into his trance and became utterly still.

He had been in that position for twenty minutes when his eyes opened. He had found what he was looking for. The answer upset him. He was delighted that he had worked things out but distressed that the name he had come up with was one of the few people he thought of as a friend. He couldn't allow himself to dwell on it, though; he needed to get back to Mayweather and Hooley to tell them what he had worked out.

Bounding down the stairs, he saw Mayweather and Major Phillip listening intently to Hooley, who had come out of the interview room again. Stepping closer, he heard the DCI complaining bitterly that Sykes was "far too tough to crumble".

They hadn't seen him but turned as one when he called out, "It's Gary Malone; we need to find him." Before anyone else could speak, he carried on. "I don't know how I could have missed it. Right from the start, he has been the only other person with access to every bit of information we were getting. More importantly, he's smart enough to have laid all the false trails.

"He's told me loads of times how he loves any game that involves deception and says he likes it that people dismiss him as a computer geek. I'd never thought about it before, but he's one of the few people who saw every bit of information that came in."

Hooley looked like a man who'd just realised he'd lost his wallet. He smacked his forehead. "Of course. Throughout this case, he's been asking questions about what we knew. Had we figured out who'd got Tricia Jenkins? What about the murdered policeman? I just put it down to overenthusiasm, but every time Jonathan popped out of the office, he was there asking me questions. It was all done under the guise of him checking to see if I needed any technical help.

"I didn't think twice. He was right at the heart of things from the start. I said he needed to look at that laptop you found at Sir James's house." He stopped. "Of course, the email exchange between Sir James and Oxford52. No wonder he kept saying how impossible it was to find out who the mystery person was. I bet it was him."

Mayweather had turned pale. "It's unbearable to think that one of our own is involved in this, let alone being the brains behind it. Jonathan, I have to ask, are you sure?"

He didn't bother to speak, just nodded. She let the tiredness show for a moment and then looked determined. "There's no point dwelling on it, there will be plenty of time to work out what went wrong later. In the meantime, we need to get hold of him. That reminds me: I don't think I've seen him today."

Hooley chipped in. "I spoke to him this morning, so he was around then. The bloody snake rang to ask if I needed any help. I just thought he was being a bit over-keen. The man's made a complete fool out of me. I'm just grateful that Jonathan worked him out. But as you say, ma'am, plenty of time for blame later. Let's get looking for him." He pointed at Major Phillips. "I suspect he'll have long gone, but let's go and check his desk."

"Be delighted to help," said the major. "My boys will be more than happy to join the hunt. In fact, I think it's safe to say it would be a pleasure."

Minutes later it was established that no one had seen Gary Malone since the morning, although one of the detectives reported that he had seen him apparently downloading files onto a flash drive.

"I wonder what information the sod's taken with him," said Hooley a short while later as a small team raced round to Malone's home address, an expensive-looking modern apartment building close to the Cromwell Road and the private Cromwell Hospital.

"I would say this is a bit beyond Mr Malone's police pay scale," said Hooley, eyeing the building from the command vehicle, which had been shifted from Mayfair. Before Roper could reply, the SAS team had breached the front door and was inside the four-bedroom apartment.

Within minutes the news came back that the place was empty. Hooley and Roper rushed to see for themselves, but the flat had been totally cleared of information. No computers and no documents.

Hooley resisted the urge to kick the walls. "I suppose it was a bit much to hope he was sitting here waiting for us," he told Roper. "At least we've got his picture being issued to all the media, so his ugly mug will be everywhere soon. And if he tries to leave the country, we'll get him."

68

It was just after 4 a.m. and Roper and Hooley were walking into work. Both men had spent a restless night, and over a 2.30 a.m. cup of tea they had agreed they would make an early start. Roper was a bundle of nervous energy. He had spent the night trying to work out where Malone might have got to. Checking in with the duty team before they set off confirmed there was still no sighting of him.

Hooley felt washed out. He had been woken several times by a nightmare where someone was hunting him in the dark. He had finally given up all hope of decent sleep at 2 a.m., when he had woken with his heart pounding and covered in cold sweat. This time he had no recollection of what the nightmare was but decided enough was enough. He took a long, hot shower, put on his dressing gown and went into the kitchen, where he found Roper filling the kettle.

Now they were on a circuitous route which would take them past a cafe that opened early. The DCI was contemplating a double-whammy of extra-strong cappuccino and a bacon sandwich with tomato sauce. It would either blast him awake or give him a heart attack. He didn't care which. Looking at Roper, who was almost bouncing with energy, he figured a glass of water might be the best thing.

Food and drink on board, they walked past the paper seller at Victoria Station. Hooley grabbed a *Daily Mail* and *The Times*. His football team had managed to progress to the semi-finals of the Champions League after a breathless encounter with the German side Bayern Munich. When he got the chance, he was going to allow himself a short break to read the match reports.

Roper sat at his desk and was rapidly absorbed into his research. Hooley placed his newspapers on the far edge of his desk. He didn't want to get distracted and started to work his way through the overnight reports. He thought about going to have a look at Mick Jones and Dan Sykes on the floor below but decided it would be better to wait for them to have breakfast, which wouldn't be for a few hours yet.

He was just prioritising the rest of the day when Mayweather appeared in the doorway. Despite the early hour she was immaculately turned out and looked as fresh as a daisy.

"You look terrible," she told him, the blow only slightly softened by the sympathetic smile that accompanied it. "I take it neither of you were able to sleep? Neither could I. I came in at two o'clock this morning because I couldn't stand sitting around at home. Since you're both in, let's have a catch-up in fifteen minutes."

Hooley gave her a thumbs up and then looked to see if Roper had been paying attention. He was surprised to see he had his head tilted forty-five degrees to the left and was looking at one of the headlines on the front of *The Times*. He had just made out that it said something about Heathrow when Roper groaned loudly.

"What's the matter?"

"I've just remembered that thing I've been trying for all night. It goes back to when I was suspended." He checked his diary for the date. "Six months and four days ago. Gary Malone said something to me. He said he'd just passed his pilot's exam and promised he would take me for a flight if I was allowed back to work.

"That was the day when I was ordered out of the building. It was a bad day for me, and I put everything out of my mind. He told me he had access to a plane at Biggin Hill. He claimed he just hired it, but I bet he bought it with the money he was making from his criminal activities."

Hooley felt all trace of tiredness vanish. Within minutes he had an armed team on their way. They were going to be dropped at Biggin Hill by helicopter and just needed to get to London Heliport in Battersea. Meanwhile, one of the duty detectives was on the phone to air traffic control asking them to stop any flights out of Biggin Hill.

"Apparently it's still early enough for flights to have only just started, so hopefully we might get him," said the detective.

Time seemed to slow, but, in reality, events were moving fast as they waited for information. Then a call came in from Biggin Hill. They had their man. Cheers erupted in the office, and people came through to shake hands with Roper, something that had never happened before.

It seems the arrest had been quite dramatic. Malone had decided to defy the no take-off call and was taxiing his Cessna 208 towards the runway. Only sharp work by a patrol car, driven flat out, had prevented him from getting airborne.

"I'd have had the bugger shot down anyway," claimed Hooley.

Arriving back at Victoria, Malone was taken none too gently to the holding cells. Upstairs the only argument was whether Roper was to be in the interrogation room asking questions or outside observing. It was decided to start him inside.

"We need to know where the women are and how many there are. Sykes is still playing silly buggers, and we're running out of time. Everything else can wait," said Mayweather, as Hooley and Roper prepared to go and talk to him.

69

Studying Malone as he sat in the interview room, Hooley noticed the IT expert was much bigger than he had remembered. He was over six feet tall and solidly built. Yet despite his bulk, he had surprisingly petite features and small hands with long fingers. He realised it was looking at his hands that had deceived him. Only now did he see how out of proportion they were to the rest of Malone's body. He had a high forehead and round face, leading him to be dubbed the "Mekon" by his colleagues. But he had been well-liked. Not only did his arrival usually sort out some technical problem, but he was always ready with a joke and a smile to put people at ease. This made the idea that he had betrayed them all even worse.

Looking at him now, wearing a white T-shirt bearing the legend "Eton Rifles", he wondered how many other crimes he'd been involved in. But the man might have been a clone of Dan Sykes with the determined way he was protecting his secrets.

Malone broke the silence. "I hope you never thought I was like you, Roper. A useless loser scared of his own shadow. I know you thought we were pals, but you were wrong. All I had to do was say, 'Hello Jonathan' and 'Wotcher Jonathan'. You were so easy to fool because no one else would even speak to you. So, the great Jonathan Roper turns out to be stupid after all."

Hooley hated this abuse being thrown at Jonathan but waited to see if Roper would stand up for himself. Which, to his delight, he did.

"Yes, I did think you were my friend, and you really fooled me. Just don't go thinking that makes you the big man. I'm easy to fool because I can't read people. It's happened to me at school and at university and now here. No big deal, I've got used to it." He leaned across the table, getting as close as he could.

"Here's a thought, though. What you should be thinking about is that it was me who worked out what you were doing." He jabbed himself in the chest. "Me. The bloke you just said was stupid. So, if I'm so stupid, then what does that make you?"

Roper stopped talking and folded his arms. Malone had gone white and looked almost shocked. Hooley was amazed and a little proud.

Hooley used Malone's evident surprise to gain leverage. "Why don't you tell us where the women are? Go easy on yourself. If you help us now, we can make sure you spend your jail time on a hospital wing where you should be safe. And you do need to talk to us, because your fellow conspirators are talking non-stop. Even Dan Sykes."

He stopped while he held the man's gaze for a moment before carrying on. "You were raping them to get them pregnant. Did that make you feel like a big man, attacking women who couldn't fight back? Apparently, some of the victims were underage, so that makes you a paedophile as well as a cold-blooded killer. So, you see, you need to talk to me if you want to stand any chance of making what's left of your miserable life at all bearable."

If Hooley was hoping this would penetrate Malone's defences, he was swiftly disappointed.

"Got any evidence to back that up, Mr Policeman? Because I don't recognise any of that. I've never raped anyone, and that bloke you mentioned, I don't know who that is. So, either you're making it all up, or all you have are the words of losers who've been intimidated into making wild allegations. A good lawyer, and I do have one, will soon make sure you can't use that in court."

The DCI's bluff had backfired. They needed some direct evidence to pull Malone into what had happened at Mount Street.

"I think you've forgotten that Tricia Jenkins was left behind. You probably thought she was dead, but she's tough, and she's going to make it through. Our forensic teams are pulling every scrap of DNA out of that basement, so I bet it won't be long before we have something on you."

Malone was sneering. "I don't know what you're talking about. I've never heard of this woman." He placed his hands on the table and stared at Hooley. "Let's put this in simple terms so you can understand. You . . . have . . . got . . . nothing. The most you are going to get me for are some breaches of the Data Protection Act. I'll be out in a few months. And, as I understand it, someone's come up with a formula that'll let us live longer. So time in the nick is nothing really."

To Hooley's surprise, Roper stood up and left the interview room. He decided to make out it was a planned break and followed him, leaving Malone staring at the door as it closed behind them.

70

Outside he caught up with Roper. "What's up? Why the sudden departure?"

"There's something right on the tip of my tongue. It's important, and it's to do with Malone. I just need a moment to work it out."

With that, he leaned against the wall, pressing his face against the cool surface. He stood quite still for several minutes. Hooley left him to it and went to get a glass of water. He walked back to find Mayweather and the major looking at the stationary Roper.

He finally came back to life, pushing himself off the wall and saying, "It's his T-shirt," before heading back into the interview room. The three officers exchanged a look. Hooley shrugged and followed him in.

Inside Roper sat straight down, crossed his arms, and stared at Malone. He had the hint of a smile on his face, and it looked like this was annoying Malone.

"Why have you got that stupid expression on your face?"

"Your T-shirt. It's just reminded me of something."

"What, that you have a total lack of style?"

Roper was really grinning now. "I'm just thinking of something you used to say. You said it so often it was almost your catchphrase. Can you work out where I'm going with this?"

Malone was squirming now, but still refusing to be drawn into saying anything. Roper took a deep breath. "'Hide things in plain sight', that's what you used to tell me. You said people never look at what's right in front of them."

Roper paused, leaning back in his chair and looking across the table. Hooley could see that the confidence was draining away from Malone by the second. Whatever it was that Roper was thinking, it looked like he was on the right track.

"Going Underground." Roper spoke so quietly it was hard to hear. Hooley thought there was something familiar about the phrase but couldn't pin it down. He looked at Roper who had his eyes glued to Malone.

"GOING UNDERGROUND." Roper's voice was shockingly loud. The interview room seemed to fill with an electricity, energising Roper and leaving Malone shocked.

"You seemed to wear that T-shirt all the time. You must have had loads of the exact same one. And that's it, isn't it? Underground? *Deep underground*, much deeper than we've been looking. There's a secret sub-basement where you've been hiding the victims." It was a statement, not a question.

Hooley could vividly recall Malone wearing a T-shirt emblazoned with "Going Underground".

Suddenly he understood what Roper was talking about and for a moment he was filled with hot rage. He leaned in towards Malone. "You were taking the piss out of all of us." Then, just as quickly as it arose, his anger died down.

He turned to Roper. "Well done, Jonathan. Let's get going and see if we're not too late to save some lives."

* * *

Minutes later they were in the back of a squad car heading for Mayfair.

As soon as they got out at Mount Street Roper ran down to the lower basement to order everyone to complete silence.

He called out a couple of times then shook his head and turned to Hooley. The DCI didn't need any prompting, just moved into the centre of the vast space. He took a deep breath and bellowed, "ARSENAL!" Roper listened carefully and then asked him to do it again.

This time he moved over to the car park area and asked Hooley to shout again, which he did, his voice starting to sound a little hoarse. Roper appeared to get his bearings and then got the DCI to yell once more. This time Roper looked like a dog on the scent as he carefully inspected the corner which housed the elevator platform. He pressed a button on the wall which raised the platform to head height before studying the ground beneath. He spotted a small metal panel placed flush to the floor and put his foot on it. Immediately there was the sound of an electric motor and a large section of the floor started dropping. It had been created so expertly there was no trace of the outline until the floor section moved. Roper slowly disappeared as the platform dropped away by almost ten feet. Facing him was a wall with a door. He pushed it open.

Inside were three young women, all unconscious and on the floor. Hooley, who had jumped on the platform as it began dropping, shouted for the paramedics.

71

To call the trial a sensation would be an understatement, but after months of bitter court battling Malone and Sykes were found guilty on counts of murder, kidnap, false imprisonment and people trafficking. Mick Jones was found guilty on accessory charges. The scientist Matt Francis remained on the run, but after his role was spelt out in court, he was dubbed "Dr Frankenstein" by the press. After hearing the unanimous jury verdict, the judge told all three men that they would be sentenced after a review of the reports, but to expect substantial prison sentences.

They were also advised that coming up with information that might reveal the whereabouts of Matt Francis, Tommy Burton and "French Pat" could help their case. But, as Hooley pointed out, Jones didn't know, and the other two weren't telling.

The three women taken from the safe room survived in hospital for two weeks but were finally overcome by infections brought on by the extreme conditions they had been kept in. This information was used in the trial by the prosecution team, who also speculated that a similar fate must have befallen other women dragged into the medical experiments.

During the course of the trial, it emerged that Sir James Taylor had found out about the sinister methods behind the production of the medicine that had cured his cancer. On the night he disappeared Malone had lured him to the east London warehouse, where he was holding a series of dogfights. Malone said it had been his idea to leave only a torso to confuse the hunt for the philanthropist. He had seemed proud as he explained it from the dock.

Tricia Jenkins was making a slow recovery from her savage injuries. Most of the bones in her face had been broken as a result of the beating she took. She explained that Sykes had attacked her as she attempted to help the three women escape.

She also suffered amnesia. For now, the damage had robbed her of any knowledge of the work she had been involved in, although experts were cautiously optimistic that she would regain her memories over time.

As they walked away from the Old Bailey, Hooley reflected on the case and the way that Roper had risen to the challenge. He had truly established himself with the Special Investigations Unit, although most people still found him difficult to deal with.

* * *

Hooley and Roper agreed to meet later for a curry in the Balti House in Pimlico. Although Roper had moved back to his own place, they both still enjoyed the food there. But he would be catching up with Hooley later. First, he was heading over to the Chelsea and Westminster hospital, where he would be visiting Tricia Jenkins. As she began her recovery, the pair were developing an unlikely friendship.

THE END

Thank you for reading this book.

If you enjoyed it please leave feedback on Amazon or Goodreads, and if there is anything we missed or you have a question about, then please get in touch. We appreciate you choosing our book.

Founded in 2014 in Shoreditch, London, we at Joffe Books pride ourselves on our history of innovative publishing. We were thrilled to be shortlisted for Independent Publisher of the Year at the British Book Awards.

www.joffebooks.com

We're very grateful to eagle-eyed readers who take the time to contact us. Please send any errors you find to corrections@joffebooks.com. We'll get them fixed ASAP.

Made in the USA
Las Vegas, NV
06 January 2022

40517010R00152